WITH CAUSE ENOUGH?

Borgo Press Books by S. Fowler Wright

Arresting Delia: An Inspector Cleveland Classic Crime Novel
The Attic Murder: An Inspector Combridge and Mr. Jellipot Classic Crime Novel
The Bell Street Murders: An Inspector Combridge and Mr. Jellipot Classic Crime Novel
Black Widow: A Classic Crime Novel
The Capone Caper: Mr. Jellipot vs. the King of Crime: A Classic Crime Novel
Crime & Co.: An Inspector Cleveland Classic Crime Novel
Dawn: A Novel of Global Warming
Dead by Saturday: An Inspector Cleveland Classic Crime Novel
The End of the Mildew Gang: An Inspector Cauldron Classic Crime Novel (Mildew Gang #3)
Four Callers in Razor Street: An Inspector Combridge and Mr. Jellipot Classic Crime Novel
The Hanging of Constance Hillier: An Inspector Cleveland Classic Crime Novel
The Jordans Murder: An Inspector Combridge and Mr. Jellipot Classic Crime Novel
The King Against Anne Bickerton: A Classic Crime Novel
The Mildew Gang: An Inspector Cauldron Classic Crime Novel (Mildew Gang #1)
Murder in Bethnal Square: An Inspector Combridge and Mr. Jellipot Classic Crime Novel
The Police and the Public
Post-Mortem Evidence: An Inspector Combridge and Mr. Jellipot Classic Crime Novel
The Return of the Mildew Gang: An Inspector Cauldron Classic Crime Novel (Mildew Gang #2)
The Rissole Mystery: An Inspector Combridge and Mr. Jellipot Classic Crime Novel
The Screaming Lake: A Lost Race Novel
The Secret of the Screen: An Inspector Combridge and Mr. Jellipot Classic Crime Novel
Three Witnesses: A Classic Crime Novel
Too Much for Mr. Jellipot: An Inspector Combridge and Mr. Jellipot Classic Crime Novel
The Vengeance of Gwa: A Fantasy of Prehistory
Was Murder Done? A Classic Crime Novel
Who Murdered Reynard? A Classic Crime Novel
The Wills of Jane Kanwhistle: An Inspector Combridge and Mr. Jellipot Classic Crime Novel
With Cause Enough?: An Inspector Combridge and Mr. Jellipot Classic Crime Novel

WITH CAUSE ENOUGH?

AN INSPECTOR COMBRIDGE AND MR. JELLIPOT CLASSIC CRIME NOVEL

by

S. FOWLER WRIGHT

WRITING AS "SYDNEY FOWLER"

The Borgo Press
An Imprint of Wildside Press LLC

MMVIII

CONTENTS

CHAPTER I.

A PRENUPTIAL SETTLEMENT

IT WAS the early summer of 1930. For nearly six months Edith Westerham had been Mr. Jellipot's stenographer, and he had had no cause for complaint, either as to the discretion of her conduct or the quality of her work.

It was about half-past four on Wednesday afternoon when the bell rang which notified her that he required her attendance.

Her room opened into the outer office, through which those who left Mr. Jellipot's room would pass out, unless he should give them exit by a private door, which he seldom did.

She rose with alacrity, and as she opened her door a young man, probably of not more than twenty-five, came out of the solicitor's room. He was not one whom it would be easy to overlook. He was tall, well-made, and handsomer than most people consider a man should be. He walked out briskly, giving no glance to the three male clerks who were at work behind the long counter at his left hand, or to the girl who stood at her half-open door, and who had paused for a moment there. But he had to walk the length of a large room while she stood sideways to him, and she had a good view, of which she made full use, her eyes following him to the door. Then she went on to take her employer's instructions.

"I remember," Mr. Jellipot said, "that you have my permission to leave at five."

"Yes," she said, as though her mind were on other things.

"Will it inconvenience you greatly if I ask you to stay for another hour?"

"Oh, I don't know. I mean, of course not, not at all."

"Miss Westerham," Mr. Jellipot asked, with his usual mildness, "are you listening to what I say?"

The young lady appeared to rouse herself from a straying mind. She looked slightly confused, which might have surprised one who knew her well, for her feelings were not normally easy to read. "I am sorry," she said. "But it really doesn't matter at all."

Mr. Jellipot was aware that she had recovered her usual alertness and self-possession as she said this. Her eyes met his directly. They were fine eyes: large, dark brown, with good brows. Mr. Jellipot may have been aware of these facts, but his mind was on the business he had to do. He began at once to instruct her with habitual lucidity.

"This document," he said, "is the draft of a settlement to be made by Lady Eleanor Cresswell upon Mr. Bruce Nolan in anticipation of marriage. Her solicitor sent it to me this morning, and I have just taken Mr. Nolan's instructions upon it. He desires certain alterations which will necessitate—"

"You mean the gentleman who has just left you?"

"Yes, it will necessitate—"

"That was Mr. Nolan who went out as I came in?"

Mr. Jellipot looked surprised at this second interruption, but it was not natural to him to be rude to any woman, even though she might be his stenographer.

"Yes, that was Mr. Bruce Nolan. Is the point of importance?"

"I thought it might have been his solicitor—or—well, someone representing him."

"I am Mr. Nolan's solicitor. As I was trying to say, the alterations proposed will involve a substantial redrafting which I shall wish to submit to Messrs. Cole and Tilson not later than ten-thirty tomorrow morning. I will dictate it now, together with the covering letter it will require."

Miss Westerham showed no further curiosity. She opened her notebook, and took down the solicitor's dictation with practised speed.

When it was finished, she returned to her own room, completed the letters on which she had been engaged, and turned to the draft settlement, which she read with a closeness which may have assisted her to avoid errors in the suggested amendments she had to type; but when these, and the covering letter, were done, she showed no haste to be gone. Mr. Jellipot left. The clerks left. The noise of the caretaker's broom could be heard in the passage. But she still remained. It seemed that she was drafting a letter which she found great difficulty in wording to her satisfaction, and which must have been of particular privacy, for, after glancing at the empty grate, she tore up the rejected drafts, and put them into her bag.

But, at last, she appeared satisfied with the wording which she had scribbled. She took some plain letter paper from her desk, and typed it quickly. "I shall miss the last post," she said, half aloud, "if I lose any more time." She wished that there should be no risk of that.

CHAPTER II.

Mr. Nolan Requires Legal Advice

MR. JELLIPOT arrived at his office at about ten minutes to ten the next day, and had not completed inspection of the morning's correspondence when he was told that Mr. Nolan had called and wished to see him.

He hesitated for a moment, feeling an impulse to say that he was too fully engaged, for there were matters of urgency on his mind, and he had given the gentleman a large part of the previous afternoon. Besides, until he had received Mr. Tilson's reply to the suggested alterations, what more could there be to discuss? But caution and courtesy combined to lead him to a different decision. After all, he could make it a short interview, if it were no more than the time-wasting call of an over-anxious man. And suppose that the lovers had quarrelled yesterday evening? Such things do occur. "Yes, show him in."

Mr. Jellipot saw at once that if it were not a lovers' quarrel of which he was to hear, it was likely to be something at least equally serious. His client's face had nothing of the smiling charm which had carried him so pleasantly through the years of his early manhood, and was now bringing in rich dividends in the form of a marriage settlement from a wealthy and lovely bride. His manner was flustered and his hand shook slightly as he held out a letter, with the words, "I had this by the morning's post. I've no idea what it means. But I thought I'd better bring it to you to deal with."

Mr. Jellipot took the letter in his usual unhurried manner. He said: "Yes?" in a tentative voice, as he opened the single quarto sheet, and read:

33 Ashfield Terrace, S.W.3.

Dear Mr. Bruce Nolan (or whatever you prefer to call yourself now),

If you will send me £200 during the next seven days, I won't say you'll never hear from me again, because I shall expect the same payment annually, but subject to that being made, which you will easily be able to afford, you will have no interference from me.

After the way you have behaved, I don't want to see you again, and it's nothing to me whom you "marry," though it hardly seems fair to her. But I suppose we most of us get, more or less, what we deserve.

Anyway, that's how it is.

If I don't hear from you, Lady Eleanor will certainly hear from me.

Edith

Mr. Jellipot read this carefully twice over, before making any remark upon it. Then he looked up to ask: "You have kept the envelope?"

"Yes, here it is."

"Probably it is of no importance. But it is evidence of its having been sent to you. It appears that the lady considers that you are worth blackmailing. Who is she?"

"I have no idea whatever."

"Really?"

"I have no recollection of having known anyone of that name since I was at preparatory school."

"Then it has the appearance of being a particularly audacious blackmailing attempt of a rather amateur kind. The writer does not give her full name, but, without that, she should be easy to trace. Accepting your assurance that you do not know her, we must suppose that a letter addressed merely to 'Edith' will come into the writer's hands. It is clearly a matter for the police."

"You mean I ought to prosecute the writer?"

"It is often a public duty to do so. But I may add that publicity does not necessarily follow. Your name would probably be suppressed, and the newspapers are particularly discreet where the prosecution of blackmailers is concerned."

"It wouldn't take much of a report to get Eleanor guessing."

"You would prefer to take no notice of it whatever?"

"If I do that, she says she'll go to Eleanor."

"Which may be no more than an idle threat. If the writer is really a stranger to you, that is the most likely presumption."

"Then what do you advise?"

"I think you had better leave this letter with me, and I will get the police to make some enquiries concerning the writer, after which we can discuss the matter again."

"We shan't be starting anything we can't stop? Not without my consent?"

"If you mean, will the police start a prosecution themselves without your consent, I think I can assure you absolutely that it would not occur. But I would add one further caution. In consulting the police, it is of the first importance to tell them everything— literally *everything* that we know. They are particularly keen on convictions of blackmailers, which are most difficult to obtain. Anything, even of a discreditable character, which is confidentially communicated to them in such a connection would be treated very much as it would be, shall I say, by your own solicitor."

"I have no doubt you are right. But what you say hardly seems to apply in this instance."

"If you are absolutely certain that the writer of the letter is a stranger to you, then it certainly does not."

"I am absolutely certain that I don't know who the writer is."

"That is what I meant, and you have put it with greater accuracy."

"Well, I can give you my word of honour on that."

"Then there is no more to be said. I will let you know immediately I have obtained any further information. The revised draft of the settlement will be in the hands of Lady Eleanor's solicitors within the next hour."

"Oh, I'm not worrying about that. We talked it over last night, and Eleanor said she'll tell Tilson to agree to what you proposed, or she'll let him know where he gets off. I'll have all her business in this office within six months."

Mr. Jellipot looked uncomfortable. "It is kind of you to suggest that," he said. "But I am already a busy man."

"Well, it's up to you."

Mr. Nolan rose. He had recovered some of his normal charm of manner as he shook hands and withdrew, with a neatly-worded assurance of Mr. Jellipot's ability to deal with any number of black-mailers of whatever kind.

Mr. Jellipot shook hands with little less than his usual cordiality, and telephoned Chief Inspector Combridge as soon as his client left.

He offered to come to Scotland Yard, but the inspector said he already had business in the city. He would be in Basinghall Street within the next hour.

CHAPTER III.

OPINIONS DIFFER

CHIEF-INSPECTOR COMBRIDGE had no claim to Mr. Jellipot's faculty of patient, exhaustive, logical analysis which had solved some problems of criminal conduct baffling to official minds. But he was equally patient in seeking facts, and in fitting them into place till a complete picture could be built up.

He listened to Mr. Jellipot's narrative without interruption, and then began to examine the letter.

"It's good quality paper," he said. "It might have come out of a professional office."

"Yes," the solicitor agreed. "It might have come out of mine."

The inspector was not concerned with fantastic improbabilities. He went on: "It's the signature of an educated woman too. One who is accustomed to use a pen."

"Yes. We may find that we are up against something which has been prepared with more ability than the first indications suggest."

"I wouldn't say that. It's more likely the woman's relying on his not daring to squeal."

"You don't believe his assertion that he has no idea who she is?"

"It's not likely, is it?"

"Perhaps not. Unless it be the work of professional blackmailers, who are relying upon his doing nothing which might jeopardise his engagement to Lady Eleanor, and the settlement he's getting from her."

"It might be that. But why should there be any risk for him?"

"The lady is said to be of a somewhat violent temper and a particularly jealous disposition. She has already broken off two engagements. There may, of course, have been good reasons. I have been told that, apart from her temper, she is a very attractive young woman. She is also extremely rich. She may have had reasons which

14

seemed good to her for doubting the motives of those who proposed to her—and she may have been right or wrong. In the present instance, those who know Mr. Nolan may have gambled on the probability that he would pay a few hundreds rather than that anything should occur to rouse her suspicions."

"Yes, that's possible. But why say that they mean to make him go on paying? After being married and getting his settlement, he wouldn't be so frightened that he'd do that. They'd have no real hold on him at all."

"I am theorising," the solicitor replied, "on most incomplete data, and I may be very far from the facts, but it appears to me that there is some basis for an opposite deduction. They might think that he would reconcile himself the more easily to a single payment if he looked forward to a time when they would come again, and he would have the pleasure of kicking them down the stairs.

"And, apart from that, you do not need me to tell you that the position would not be as simple for him as it is now, after one payment has been made. It is too near to a confession of guilt for those who pay once to gather courage easily to resist further demands."

"Yes. And they mostly *are* guilty too. There may be cases of innocent men being blackmailed. I've no doubt there are. But I can't say that they've come my way."

"No, they are the exceptions, no doubt. And we may have come on one of them in this case."

"I'll keep an open mind about that. At any rate until I've found out who Edith is. I daresay Crabtree will know something about her."

Superintendent Crabtree had made a special study of blackmailing in all its branches. He had a wide knowledge of those who practised it habitually, including some who had been too astute to come into the hands of the police. If this were the work of any regular practitioners, it was probable that he could not merely identify them, but give valuable guidance as to the procedure they would be likely to follow.

But when Combridge saw the Superintendent an hour later, he could give no assistance beyond expressing a decided opinion that the letter was the work of an amateur hand.

"You'll find," he said confidently, "that it's from a woman he's let down. She won't have done anything to cover her tracks, and she probably won't admit she's done anything wrong. It's her sort who are the easiest to catch, and the least worth catching.

"Of course, that sort of thing ought to be stopped, though I've had cases where I'd rather have seen the other party put in the dock.

You'll find it an easy case to solve, though it will end in smoke, for Nolan won't prosecute. All you'll be able to do is to warn her off, and you'll have had the satisfaction of helping a cad."

With such comfort as could be derived from this confident opinion, Chief Inspector Combridge went at about seven o'clock that evening to make enquiries at 33 Ashfield Terrace, which, as he had already ascertained from the house agents, was occupied by Mrs. Corelli, the English widow of an Italian, who let it out in service rooms. He went with the intention of interviewing the residents there to whatever extent might be necessary to enable him to identify the writer of the letter, but after a short talk with Mrs. Corelli, he came away. He had obtained the information he required without difficulty, and he had become an astonished and thoughtful man.

CHAPTER IV.

MR. JELLIPOT IS SURPRISED

"YOU LOOK," Mr. Jellipot said, "as though you are about to tell me something of greater gravity than I was expecting to hear."

"I don't know about that. I think you will be surprised."

"Well, I often am. But why should I be surprised now? It is a matter on which I have a most open mind."

"You remember saying that the paper that letter was written on might have come from this office? Well, suppose it did?"

"We will suppose it if you wish. But on what grounds? It is obviously improbable and would, I suppose, be very difficult to prove if it were true.

"You may not know that Whitaker's sell that paper to a large proportion—probably a large majority—of the professional offices within a quarter of a mile of this street."

"I daresay they do. But would Miss Westerham have access to those supplies, as she has to yours?"

"Does the question arise? Combridge, if you would tell me what you have found out—or what you surmise, which may not be quite the same thing—in a straightforward manner, you might be saving your time and mine."

"Well, that's soon done. Number 33 Ashfield Terrace is let out in service rooms. Mrs. Corelli, an Englishwoman, widow of an Italian, is the proprietress. She answered questions frankly and seems reliable. She gave me a list of the lodgers. Mostly men. The only woman named Edith among them is Edith Westerham, a stenographer. Mrs. Corelli volunteered the information that she works for a solicitor named Jellipot in Basinghall Street."

"Well, I am certainly surprised. It would deserve the word as a mere matter of coincidence, if Miss Westerham had nothing to do with the matter. Did you get any particulars from Mrs. Corelli concerning Miss Westerham's private life or friendships?"

"She says that the girl has always been reticent about personal affairs. 'One as keeps herself to herself.' But yesterday she made a curious request which may have some connection with the matter. She said that a letter might be arriving for a Mrs. Lingfield, and asked that it should be given to her. She said that Mrs. Lingfield was a friend for whom she had agreed to take the letter in. The normal procedure is that the postman puts all the letters into a box, of which Mrs. Corelli has the key, and she takes them out and distributes them among racks in the hall, which are numbered to correspond with the rooms."

Mr. Jellipot had had time to consider the position while this explanation proceeded. Now he gave facts for facts: "Miss Edith Westerham is my stenographer. I have had her for about six months. I took her from the Townsend Secretarial Bureau without references other than their recommendation. She has been satisfactory in every way. The night before last she typed a document from which she would have learnt the particulars which are the basis of the letter. That she wrote it is a reasonable presumption, though it is not proved."

"It is impossible to defend. It is almost impossible to explain. It is possible that it is nothing worse—or better—than a practical joke. She used her own address, and must have known—if she considered the matter at all—that enquiry would be certain discovery. It is exceedingly difficult to imagine any plausible explanation.

"If she wrote the letter as a practical joke, she would want to see what the reply would be. She couldn't get it without giving her address. She may have thought that she concealed her identity sufficiently, in a house full of people, by giving only her Christian name."

"Then she must be an extremely foolish young woman. But we shall get no further forward till we hear what she has to say. I propose to ask her for an explanation at once, as I am clearly entitled to do. If you would like to be present, I think that, as I have consulted you on that matter, it would be a request I could not refuse."

Chief Inspector Combridge would have liked a little more time to consider the expediency of this step. He might have preferred to have a talk with Bruce Nolan first, and perhaps arrange for the money to be offered in a room in which he would be concealed, so that he could step out to arrest her when her guilt would be beyond denial.

But Mr. Jellipot had already touched the bell which communicated with the stenographer's room. In a moment, she might appear. He could not prevent her employer's questioning her, and, if that were to be done, he certainly would like to hear her replies. But he had another doubt. However keen the hunt for a criminal may be, it must be done according to rules. He said: "She ought not to be cautioned, if you're going to—"

"I'm not going to take a statement from her, if you mean that. All I want is the truth. I shall tell her who you are and she can refuse to explain, if she likes. It's just possible that she can't—that she knows nothing about it, though that's hard to think. If so, she is directly concerned in finding out what the explanation is. You can keep entirely silent, if you prefer."

Feeling that he was being rushed, but that matters were beyond his control, Combridge said no more. After all, Mr. Jellipot was an experienced lawyer, and the matter concerned the discipline of his own office, apart from its larger issues. And by this time Miss Westerham was in the room.

CHAPTER V.

MISS WESTERHAM EXPLAINS

THE girl came into the room, notebook in hand, and sat down in her usual chair. It happened frequently that she was summoned to take dictation in a client's presence, and she scarcely glanced at the detective officer as she waited for Mr. Jellipot to begin.

But when he did speak, her expression quickly changed. The inspector, watching closely, saw the sudden pallor of her face as Mr. Jellipot came to the point at once.

"There is a letter here on my desk which Mr. Bruce Nolan received yesterday morning. This is Chief Inspector Combridge from Scotland Yard, who is making enquiries concerning it. You will therefore understand that anything you say is being communicated to the police. The letter makes use of confidential information which came to your knowledge in the course of your duties here. It bears your address. Its purport is to demand money with threats. It is signed with your Christian name. Is there anything that you wish to say?"

"I wrote it, if that's what you want to know. But I didn't think he'd be such a fool."

"To whom do you refer?"

"Mr. Bruce Nolan, if that happens to be his real name."

"I can assure you it is. You mean you thought he'd pay the money rather than risk a scandal?"

"I didn't know what he'd do. I thought he'd come to try to talk me over, more likely than not, or to get better terms. But even he'd have needed some cheek for that. I didn't think he'd go to the police."

"May I ask why not?"

"Well, it's not what I wanted to happen. It's no good to me, and it must be ruin to him when it all comes out, as I suppose it will now. No, I didn't think he'd be such a fool."

"When what comes out?"

"That he's married to me."

"You have proof of that?"

"Well, we've got a child."

Mr. Jellipot did not make the obvious reply that parenthood is no proof of marriage. He went on as though assuming that her assertions were true.

"Do I understand rightly that, knowing that he was married to you, you would have kept silence while he went through the pretence of marriage with another woman, if you were paid to do so?"

"I shouldn't put it that way. He owes me something, doesn't he?"

"I should require to know much more than I do now before I could answer that. But so long as you were paid the sum you mentioned, you would have allowed his marriage to Lady Eleanor to take place without disclosing that you are his wife already? Is that what you wish me to believe?"

"Yes, I should have been glad."

"Why?"

"Because it would have been best all round. If no one knew, what was the harm? He wouldn't have let it out after marrying her. And I should have been free. If you look at it sensibly, that's how it would have worked. But now he's gone to the police, I should say he's in the soup, and it's just what he deserves."

"I am afraid it is your own position you have to consider, rather than his. Can you tell me when and where the marriage took place?

"Yes, of course. It was June 22nd, 1927, at the Marylebone Registrar's."

"You have the certificate?"

"No, Harry kept that."

"Who was he?"

"That was what he called himself then. Harry Lingfield."

"Then your real name is Mrs. Lingfield?"

"Yes, unless he gave a false name, as I suppose he did. I don't know what it would be then."

"It is a reasonable qualification. But as you are probably aware, a false name does not invalidate such a marriage, if it be regular in other particulars."

"Well, I wish it did."

Mr. Jellipot became silent for a long minute, during which the inspector thought of several questions he would like to put, but had the discretion to maintain a difficult silence. Then Mr. Jellipot said: "The matter which appeared serious before has assumed additional gravity as a result of the statements which you have made. For the moment you had better go back to your work, while I discuss with Chief Inspector Combridge what the next step shall be."

Mrs. Lingfield (if that were really her legal name) rose but seemed in no haste to go. She looked as though there were other things she would like to say. But like the inspector she controlled her disposition to further speech and went slowly out of the room.

She had scarcely closed the door when the inspector began: "You're going to keep that girl on?"

"No, I have not decided to do so. I should think it's highly improbable. Apart from the more serious aspects of the case, she has betrayed her trust to myself in a manner which would be very difficult to overlook. But it is not a matter in which I should act in haste."

"You believe her tale?"

"Do you?"

"I don't know what to think."

"Neither do I. I conclude that either she or Nolan is a particularly cool and audacious criminal. There is no escaping from that. The question is which, and it is one on which we should not risk a mistake. I should be disposed to believe her largely on the ground that no woman of ordinary intelligence would hope to sustain such a tale if it were false, but for one overriding objection. If Bruce Nolan had really married her and were now proposing to commit bigamy, is it conceivable that he would have brought her letter to me, and consented to my suggestion that it should be passed onto you?"

"That's how it looks to me, but it's a queer world. I thought you might have asked her a bit more that you did."

"And I was not sure that I ought not to give her an opportunity of being separately advised. But the decisive reason was that if she talked for a year she could not have said substantially more than she had already. It seems to me that the next step must be to inform Nolan of the assertions that she has made.

"If he admits their truth, his own position will be too discreditable—I should say too criminal—to allow of his prosecuting her; if he maintain that they are false, he is bound to take action; should he bring a jury to that view, she will have made her position immensely worse by the allegations she has made against him. It was in view of that possibility that I wondered whether she ought not to be given an opportunity of having separate advice.

"I propose to get Nolan here this afternoon, and that we see him together."

The inspector said that nothing would suit him better than that.

CHAPTER VI.

MR. NOLAN IS QUITE SURE

MR. NOLAN shook hands with Mr. Jellipot and was introduced to Chief Inspector Combridge by whom his charming smile was not warmly reciprocated, for the red-headed and somewhat blunt-nosed detective officer had a prejudice against handsome men.

Ignoring this lack of cordiality, Nolan took charge of the conversation before Mr. Jellipot's more leisurely method had come into action. Mr. Jellipot did not mind that. He was always willing to listen. He knew that it is the listener, not the talker, who learns.

"I've been thinking this over," Mr. Nolan began, "and I've decided that, if you've been able to find the woman who wrote that letter and have warned her of the kind of mess she'll be in if she tries to make trouble with Eleanor, I should be rather a fool not to leave it there.

"I suppose I might prosecute without Eleanor's hearing about it, but it seems an off chance to me, and that's the only angle from which I'm concerned about it in any way. But for her, I should probably have just thrown the letter onto the fire and wondered at the folly of anyone wasting the price of a stamp on so silly an attempt. You see," he added, turning to Combridge with a pleasant modulation of voice, as though he were giving him information of a particularly confidential character, "Lady Eleanor is inclined to be just a little unreasonable where other women are concerned, and I have to take that into account. If she should hear that I were prosecuting a woman on such grounds, it might be just as difficult to convince her that there was nothing in it as if the woman were to go with some lie to her. And whatever threats she may make, I don't see that she'd gain anything by that apart from the warning she's had from you."

"I can't say I have warned her so far," Combridge answered with some irritation, being less patient than Mr. Jellipot at having the conversation taken out of their hands in such a manner. "I don't say that I should have adopted that course under other circumstances, but the fact is that the position has developed in an unexpected way."

Mr. Jellipot spoke for the first time: "I don't think you can usefully discuss what course you will be wise to take till you know the full facts, as we have them now. In the first place, I have an explanation to give you and an apology to offer. You may have wondered through what channel the negotiation of the proposed settlement, or other relevant circumstances, became known to your correspondent. The fact is that she is a stenographer in this office and abused the confidential knowledge which came to her in that capacity."

"You mean that she's here with you!" There was no doubt of the depth of astonishment that this information caused. The inspector, watching keenly and wishing that a different method had been pursued, that Nolan had been confronted with the lady who claimed so intimate a connection with him, thought that for a second there was an appearance of consternation also; but if so, it was too transient for certainty, and it is easy to imagine that which we look to see.

"Yes, I regret to say that that is the fact," Mr. Jellipot replied. "I must also tell you that the lady makes an assertion which, should she persist in it, would render it impossible in my judgement for you to contract the marriage which you now contemplate without first taking legal action against her. In a word, she asserts that she is your wife."

"That's laying it on a bit thick."

"She says precisely that she was married to you, in the name of Harry Lingfield, at the Marylebone Registrar's Office on June 22nd, 1927."

"That might be anyone. She hasn't really had the cheek to say that she was married to me?"

"Not in your own name. The matter might be disposed of, one way or the other, very much more easily if she had."

"I expect she's too fly for that."

"It is a legitimate contention."

Mr. Jellipot knew that there was more than one blackmailing gang operating in London, well financed and controlled by astute, far-seeing men, adroit both to lay cunning plots for foolish or culpable victims and to avoid the penalties of the law. What better place could there be than a solicitor's office in which to obtain the kind of knowledge which their operations required? What better method could there be than to introduce a stenographer to such an office as his? And how could such an introduction be effected without the inconveniences of references through a better medium than that of a secretarial bureau? He saw that they must have a girl of the appearance and capacity which the part required, and then send her for a secretarial training which she might not require, so that she would be recommended in good faith for a confidential position. He blamed himself more keenly than before that he had engaged her with no greater precautions. He had always contemned references, preferring his own judgment of appearance and manner, of voice and the spoken word. But, of course, they would select one who would be expert to speak and act so that confidence would be won.

Still, would it be good policy to use such an opportunity to act as Miss Westerham—or whatever her name might be—was now doing? Whatever other results it might have, would it not end her usefulness as a procuress of the confidential knowledge which she might have passed on to her employers for their evil uses for years to come? Surely it would have been sounder to keep the two roles apart? But perhaps there was a limit to the number of ladies available for these diverse, but equally essential parts? ...

Such were the doubts that passed through the solicitor's very open and scrupulously logical mind during a long minute of silence, for Chief Inspector Combridge had decided to listen rather than to attempt to lead the course of the conversation, being uncertain of what part it might be necessary for the police ultimately to take; and Bruce Nolan was also facing a position which had given him cause for thoughts of a very different kind.

Mr. Jellipot spoke again: "The issue is at least one about which there can be no ambiguity on your side. On hers, the possibility of mistaken identity might conceivably arise. But when she says she is married to you, and you say you are unmarried and do not know her at all, you cannot be mistaken in what you say. Should you like me to call her in?"

Combridge's eyes were on Nolan's face as this question was asked, for he considered that he provided the most doubtful element of the problem. He did not doubt that it was a case of blackmailing, on which point he considered that the letter spoke for itself. But he knew that the guilt of Edith Westerham did not imply the innocence of Bruce Nolan. Most of the blackmailed men who had to be coaxed into prosecuting and protected from hostile publicity like hothouse flowers were of a vicious or criminal type. The less usual feature of this case was that the blackmailer asserted that she herself was the victim rather than one into whose hands documents or knowledge had come concerning an event which she did not share; and that

augmented the probability that her assertions had at least some substance of fact. But probability is not proof.

Now he thought that he saw again that momentary shadow of
fear which he had imagined or noticed before. But again—if it were
not imagination—it was too slight and transient for any certain deduction to be founded upon it. Then the naturally harassed man
looked at Mr. Jellipot with a smile by the charm of which few men
and fewer women would be entirely uninfluenced. "It is a matter,"
he said, "on which I should be guided by you entirely."

Mr. Jellipot could not object to that. He was Mr. Nolan's solicitor in other matters, if not precisely in the unexpected issue that had
arisen. But it was just that fact which made him slow to reply. Was
it wise to confront the two in the presence of a police officer? To get
at the truth, probably yes. In Nolan's interest? That must largely depend upon what the truth might be. Anyway, it was a responsibility
he would not take till he should be better informed, or his position
should be clearer than it now was.

"Then," he said, "I think, for the moment, I will withdraw the
suggestion. Instead of that, I will give you some advice which may
not be easy to follow, but I believe you will find it to be sound, on
the presumption—and only on the presumption—that you are a
stranger to Miss Westerham."

Mr. Nolan spoke readily now. He may be said to have interrupted the solicitor's leisurely periods, to interject: "I give you my
word of honour on that. I cannot say that I have never met the lady.
How could I? But I say emphatically that I have never married anyone, at Marylebone or anywhere else, and I have not the least idea
who the young woman is."

"Then my advice is this. It is not a matter on which it would be
wise for me to represent you, particularly in view of the fact that the
allegation comes from someone in my employment. Next to myself,
Lady Eleanor's solicitors are most conversant with the whole position, and she, from a different angle, is almost as nearly concerned
in clearing it up as you are yourself. If you go to them and lay the
whole position frankly before them, it is a confidence which they
can hardly fail to appreciate, and may largely influence the advice
which they will in any case almost certainly be giving Lady Eleanor
upon it before many days are past.

"At the same time, you should tell her everything, including that
you have gone to them. If you take that course, you may win her
confidence and support, which you will naturally wish to have."

"What will be done with the letter?"

"You will give it to them yourself."

"Very well, I'll do that."

Mr. Nolan rose, shook hands with smiling cordiality both with Mr. Jellipot and the representative of the detective police, and went out to follow the advice he had received.

Chief Inspector Combridge also rose. "It's Marylebone for me," he remarked. "And after that—"

"After that we shall be about where we are now, unless Miss Westerham has told a lie which could not fail to be promptly exposed—and that is too much to hope."

"Well, we've got to find out. But I think we should have kept the letter."

"It is Mr. Nolan's property. In any case, it will be quite safe in the hands of Cole and Tilson."

"Yes. I suppose so. I'll probably be seeing you again tomorrow. Going to keep the girl on?"

"It would be an improbable assumption. But I shall have another talk with her before I decide anything finally."

The inspector went, and Mr. Jellipot looked along his shelves to refresh his memory upon the law of blackmail, after doing which he said aloud: "Well, we have to take the law as it is. But I wonder what Patience would say to that."

Then he rang for Miss Westerham.

CHAPTER VII.

MR. JELLIPOT TAKES ADVICE

MR. JELLIPOT did not go home when he left his office. He had an appointment to dine with Miss Patience Manly at the Waldorf that evening.

Miss Manly was a lady of somewhat less than his own years, a member of the Society of Friends, and of a robust vitality. This vitality, by a natural law, did something to reduce her apparent age, but in doing this it had no assistance from her. She was of sound and lively mind, and a directness of downright speech which Mr. Jellipot did not fail both to admire and enjoy, though it contrasted with his own qualified discretions.

Their acquaintance, which had ripened into a friendship of increasing intimacy, had begun in the improbable atmosphere of a bizarre murder in the quiet village of Jordans.[1] It was now habitual, when she came into town for a day's shopping or to attend one of the rather numerous committees on which she sat, to telephone the solicitor, so that they could arrange to dine together before she returned to the sober dignity of her Jordans home.

"Edward," she said, as soon as she had ordered the meal (for that was a matter which he had learned the advantage of leaving to her), "you have something more than the usual business preoccupations upon your mind."

"That is so," he replied. "It is a story which cannot properly be told in a few words. But if it will not weary you, I should particularly value your opinion upon it."

Miss Manly smiled. "I don't suppose I shall go to sleep. But is it anything relating to a client's affairs?"

"Yes, it is a serious—almost certainly criminal—and extraordinary affair. One of two parties (a young woman) is an unscrupulous

---

[1] See *The Jordans Murder*.

and audacious criminal, or the other (a man to whom she says she is married) is contemplating bigamy with an equal disregard of the penal consequences involved."

"A woman wouldn't be likely to say she was married to a man of that sort, if it weren't true."

"It is not as simple as that. There is a question of blackmail also."

"It sounds interesting." Miss Manly's very blue eyes—the attractive feature of a plain face—were directed disconcertingly upon her companion as she added with a humorous smile: "I remember you once told me what you thought of a solicitor who discussed his client's affairs with his wife."

"But you are not my wife. There is no parallel whatever."

Mr. Jellipot's protest was made with more haste than he usually showed, and it might have been difficult to find any living person who had seen him look as confused as he did next moment.

He was aware at once that there was no sense in what he had said, and he was acutely conscious that he had brought a subject on which he spent much anxious debate into the forefront of his mind, and perhaps of hers.

Should he ask her to marry him, what would her answer be? Should she consent, and would it be a matter for future congratulation or regret?

They were both of settled habits, of mature years, used to freedom in the control of their own homes.

Probably she would refuse, with a kindly word and a characteristic smile. But would she add that their friendship had better end? He would regret that. His acquaintances were many, his friendships few.

Another thought had troubled him much of late. Was he acting in an unseemly manner by developing the acquaintance for so long a time without making such a proposal?

He had not lived for fifty observant years without realising that many women would expect an offer of marriage under such circumstances, or that affirmative replies are frequently given.

Patience Manly's eyes did not leave his face, and he might have been even more disconcerted had he known how exactly she read his thoughts. What she said was: "Oh well, if that's clear to you! Anyway, go ahead."

"The matter," Mr. Jellipot said, with a quick return to the verbal precision and logical adroitness which were normal to him, "is not solely that of a client. In addition to the fact that it is one on which I have already advised him, and he has agreed to instruct another firm, there is the troublesome circumstance that a member of my office staff is involved, and I am not entirely certain that developments may not follow in which I should myself be the defendant in a legal action."

"Then someone will be asking for trouble. I can give you that opinion without waiting to hear the facts. But I'm getting really curious to know what they are."

With this encouragement, Mr. Jellipot narrated them with a lucid brevity which yet took him far through the course of a somewhat neglected meal before he came to the point at which he had called Miss Westerham into his office that afternoon.

"I told her," he said, "that she would be wise to say nothing more, whatever the truth might be, until she had listened carefully to what I had to say to her.

"I then told her that, even if she were Nolan's wife, it did not justify her in taking the course she did. When she saw him in my office she was, of course, free to assert her relationship, but not to use information of a confidential character subsequently acquired. She should have reported the whole matter to me."

"I don't say you were wrong. But still, when a woman—"

"Anyway, that is what I said. I went on to explain the law of criminal libel as it applied to such a letter as she had written—to the demanding of money by menace in any form—and I warned her of the almost certain consequences should she persist in her statements, if they were not true. I pointed out that, unless they were immediately withdrawn, a searching enquiry must be made, which would be certain to expose their falsity, and that while her position, after such a confession, might be very serious, she would have taken the only possible course to mitigate, if not to avert, the legal peril in which she lay.

"On the other hand, if she had said no more than the truth, I should be able, without justifying what she had written, to take a widely different view, and would be disposed to consider to what extent I could assist her to obtain her undoubted rights."

"She kept quiet while you said all that?"

"Absolutely. Then she asked me a question: 'Do you think I *want* to be married to that cad?' And I replied that I wished in the first place to have a direct statement of the facts of the case, and we could then discuss any questions arising therefrom. After that we talked for a long time, but, in a word, she persists that her tale is true. I may add that the details she gave make it more improbable than it sounded before."

"How was that?"

"She asserts that the circumstances of the marriage, and of some subsequent cohabitation which took place, were such that they may be less easy to prove than would be supposed."

"It sounds as though she got into the hands of a very cunning rogue."

"It is open to that explanation. It is also true that, if the whole story be a concocted plot, that is exactly the nature of the defence which would be set up."

"But you believe her?"

"She either told me the truth—more or less—or she is one of the most accomplished liars I have ever encountered in twenty-five years of legal practice. But as to that, it must not be overlooked that, if she be a professional blackmailer, she will certainly be an expert actress. And it may be added that women are commonly more skilful liars than men."

"You really think that?"

"I did not intend to imply that their standard of truth is lower. That would be a generalisation on which I would hesitate. But, on the average, they are less clumsy than men."

"So it was a compliment? What do you intend to do now?"

"I am undecided. I told her I would consider and let her know in the morning, when she is to come into the office to clear up her work."

"So you have sacked her?"

"I thought it inexpedient to retain her services, for more reasons than one."

"Has she any means of living?"

"I told her that she would be paid a month's salary when she comes in tomorrow."

"Then you did believe her?"

"That would be going too far. She says that she is without means and that she has a child to support. It is a risk that I could not take."

"No, you wouldn't. I should rather like to see this young woman. I've never met a real blackmailer. Not one on the active list, anyway."

"It is what I hoped you would say. I thought you might get at the truth more surely than I feel able to do."

"You mustn't depend on that."

"It is my best hope."

"Well, I'll have a try. You think she'll come?"

"Not certainly. She may have seen that the game was up and have gone into hiding. In some ways it would be the best end of the matter for which we could hope."

"It would go far towards clearing Nolan."

"It would go all the way. And I should be glad of that."

"All the way?"

"Yes. I think so. Her tale was circumstantial about the child, which she says is boarded in Devonshire. I have the alleged address."

"Yes, I see what you mean. Though—"

"There are almost always qualifications. We may put that aside. You will come to Basinghall Street in the morning?"

"Yes. About eleven."

"I told her that you would be unlikely to be earlier than that."

"You *told* her?"

"As a possibility only. I did not, of course, mention your name."

"Well, I'll do what I can. But we'd better be moving now, or I shall miss the train I said I'd be on. It's my turn for the bill."

Mr. Jellipot did not contest that. It was in accordance with a bargain they had made when these evening meetings had shown signs of a regular frequency. Miss Manly had said that for him always to pay was an assertion of the inferiority of women, which she would not lightly admit.

Actually, they both had that indifference to money which is possible only to those to whom it comes in sufficient quantity without anxious effort, and to whom cupidity is an unnatural vice.

CHAPTER VIII.

"MRS. NOLAN WILL STAY WITH ME"

CHIEF INSPECTOR COMBRIDGE called upon Mr. Jellipot next morning. He said: "I found out this much, and it supports the girl's tale as far as it goes, but you'll say that's no great distance. A woman who gave the name of Edith Westerham was certainly married to a man who gave the name of Henry Lingfield on the date she says. The witnesses to the marriage were Connie Jones, who is dead (she was a professional witness, known to the registrar's officer), and a Lucille Belloes, who ought to help if she can be found.

"Of course, the registrar doesn't remember what they looked like, nor anyone else there. It isn't likely he would. Then there are the signatures. There may be some help in them.

"But what I'd like to know is where they went after they were married. Nolan isn't a man that people would forget or mistake. Not if he's stayed in their house. Even with a hotel, there'd be a good chance. But I expect she'll say he left her at once."

"On the contrary, she says that they were together for between three and four weeks. But there may be difficulties for all that."

"Still got her with you?"

"She is leaving this morning. At present, Miss Manly is with her."

"Miss Manly? Oh, I see. You've called her in to help. Well, I'd say she'd get at the truth if anyone could."

"I should value her opinion as to the girl's veracity. I wouldn't go beyond that."

"You believe her tale?"

"I am in grave doubt. I would like to believe both Nolan and her, which is impossible. But it appears probable that she will stand her ground."

"Then Nolan will have to prosecute."

"He certainly will, if he still intends to marry Lady Eleanor. Or, we might say, anyone else. I suppose you will offer to conceal his name in the usual way?"

"I expect we shall."

"It is a monstrous injustice."

Chief Inspector Combridge was not infrequently startled by the solicitor's opinions on the law which in different ways they both served, but he had rarely been more than he was now.

He said bluntly: "I don't see what you mean by that. If we didn't, we couldn't get blackmailers run in at all."

"Probably not. And to discourage blackmail is a most meritorious end. But should not both names be protected equally?"

"Cover up the blackmailer's name? We don't think helping that scum is any business of ours."

"Naturally not. But is it not a principle of English law that an accused person is considered innocent till conviction is obtained?"

"Well, that might apply to everyone we round up."

"So it should. The question of whether the name of any accused person should be published *without his own consent* is a large one, and there is much to be said upon either side. But that proceedings should take place at which the name of one party is published and that of the other withheld is contrary to the spirit of equity. Or so it appears to me."

"Well, we don't do it for that."

Mr. Jellipot did not pursue the subject further. He said: "Perhaps before you leave you would like me to ascertain whether Miss Manly has learnt anything which she thinks you should know."

"Yes, that suits me."

Mr. Jellipot took up the receiver. He said: "I should like a word with Miss Manly, if she's still in Miss Westerham's room. Very well, bring it in."

He turned to the inspector to explain: "Miss Manly and Miss Westerham have gone out together. Miss Manly has left a note for me."

Next moment a clerk brought it in. It was an unfolded half sheet of paper. He read in Miss Manly's rather bold writing: "Mrs. Nolan is coming home with me, where she will stay unless I let you know otherwise. Perhaps you will telephone me this evening."

Mr. Jellipot passed it without comment to the detective officer who whistled as he read it.

"Mrs. Nolan!" he said. "That means the young woman's pulled it off with her. We're going to see the feathers fly in this case."

"You may possibly be assuming somewhat beyond the fact," Mr. Jellipot replied cautiously. "Miss Manly may be doing no more than giving her the benefit of a doubt which we all have."

Inspector Combridge was unmoved by this characteristically cautious view. "Well," he said, "that's how it looks to me." He got up to go.

CHAPTER IX.

MR. NOLAN FOLLOWS ADVICE

MR. TILSON read a letter he did not like. It said:

Dear Charles,

Will you please pass the settlement deed as Bruce's lawyer wishes it to be.

It was nice of you to telephone me, and I know you think you have to look after my interests. But I want Bruce to really *be* independent in money matters, so that he won't ever feel awkward about it afterwards. You know it makes no real difference to me.

Do understand.

Sincerely,

E.

"If the man weren't such a bounder—" he muttered angrily, and then drew his long legs from under his desk and strolled into the senior partner's room. "What," he asked, "do you think of this?"

Mr. Cole, a small, round, rubicund man, with little outward indication of his profession beyond the piercing shrewdness of twinkling eyes, took the letter and read it with one rapid glance.

"Speaking to 'Dear Charles'," he said, "I can only ask: What did you expect to get? Speaking to a partner in the firm, I must congratulate you on having received a most satisfactory letter."

"Oh, rot! If he weren't the worst bounder of the three—"

36

"Charles, there have been times when I have wondered whether any man who proposed to marry that lady would obtain your approval."

"What do you think of him yourself?"

"He is not a type I admire. He is an obvious fortune-hunter. It does not follow that he is not sincerely in love with an attractive girl. Do you think it *particularly* extraordinary that anyone should be in love with Lady Eleanor?"

As he spoke, a clerk entered and laid some letters on the senior partner's desk. Observing that Mr. Tilson was in the room, he said: "Mr. Nolan has just called, sir. He said he wants to see you on urgent business. He'll wait if you are engaged."

"I wonder," Tilson exclaimed irritably, "what the devil it is now! In any case, he's got his own lawyer. He's got no business to come to me. Tell him he'd better see Mr. Jellipot, and he can give me a ring."

The clerk returned with this message, and Charles Tilson answered his partner's question in a tone which gave evidence that the interruption had not improved his temper.

"Of course I'm not such a fool as that. The trouble is that, with all the money she's got, she only hooks onto the wrong men."

"That's because they all look at it the same way."

"I don't know what on earth you mean."

"I mean that if one poor man proposes to a girl simply because she's got money, and another doesn't for the same reason, there's not much to choose between them."

"You mean there's nothing to choose between a decent man and a cad?"

"I mean they're both putting the money before the girl."

Charles made no answer to that. He went back to his own room where he received a further message from Nolan, who had declined to leave. He wished Mr. Tilson to know that it was with Mr. Jellipot's knowledge that he had called.

"Well," he said, "show him in."

If Bruce Nolan were aware of the dislike which he aroused in the solicitor's heart, it made no difference to the urbanity of his outward manner. His expression was grave and troubled, as was suitable to the occasion on which he came, but that did not diminish the charm of his usual smile as he said affably: "I was afraid you'd think I was butting in where I'd no business to be. It was natural you should. But I haven't come about the settlement. I leave that to you and Jellipot.

"It's something more serious, though it's so absurd that I find it hard to take it in that way. But Mr. Jellipot agreed that it was something you—and, of course, Lady Eleanor—ought to know, and, when I tell you about it, you'll understand why he can't deal with it himself. In a word, a woman—one whom, as far as I know, I never met in my life—says I married her a year or two ago in another name."

"Has it any substance of truth at all?"

"None whatever."

"If a strange woman molests you with such a tale, I should advise you to hand her over to the police."

"She has not molested me personally, but I received this letter."

Mr. Tilson read the letter. He observed in a reluctant mind the frankness of Nolan's attitude in informing him of it. He said: "It looks like a rather audacious—and clumsy—blackmailing attempt. But there is no clear assertion of marriage here. I conclude that something more has happened since you had it.

"I appreciate your action in informing us of what is occurring, but I see no reason why Mr. Jellipot should not deal with it. In such a matter I should say that you could not easily be better advised."

"The point is that the blackmailer is his own stenographer."

Mr. Tilson was clearly astonished at this information, but his mind grasped its implications with trained rapidity. "You mean me to understand that she stands up to this assertion?"

"So Mr. Jellipot says. I have not seen her myself. He advised me not to."

"On what grounds?"

"He didn't say that."

"Is there any suggestion that she is *non compos mentis*?"

"I don't know about that. I had instructed him to set the police onto it before we knew who she was. They seem to be more inclined to suspect that it is the work of a blackmailing gang."

"Whom do you mean by they?"

"It was Chief Inspector Combridge I saw."

"He is a most experienced officer. Do I understand that you want us to act for you in this matter?"

"I should be very glad if you would."

"I think I must discuss it with Mr. Jellipot before giving you a final answer. Suppose you look in tomorrow about this time? And do you wish us to inform Lady Eleanor, or would you rather do it yourself?"

"I intend to do it when I see her this evening."

"Well, you seem to be dealing with an annoying matter in the right way. But if the woman is a stranger to you, I should say you have no reason to be greatly concerned."

It was a verdict of approval which had additional value as coming from lips which found no pleasure in speaking Bruce Nolan's praise. When he had gone, Tilson went again to his partner's room and told him of this unexpected development.

"So," Mr. Cole commented, with twinkling eyes, "you are to save the young lady from contracting a bigamous marriage? She ought to be grateful to you for that."

"I wish I knew what the truth is."

"Naturally. But there's not much doubt that we soon shall. It sounds like blackmail to me. If it is no more than that, it's a safe guess that your lovely client will be Lady Eleanor Nolan within six months from now. But if it's not—well, I should say that five minutes on the phone with Jellipot will give you a good idea of what the last act's likely to be."

CHAPTER X.

A More Difficult Interview

MR. TILSON spent a few minutes in mentally reviewing the surprising information he had received. He looked up a point of law on which he would not have liked to show hesitation to another solicitor. Then he rang up Mr. Jellipot.

He received a concise statement of facts, given with Mr. Jellipot's usual exactness, but adding little to what he had been told previously. He said: "Perhaps I'd better come round and see you? Say in about half an hour?"

"That is as you like. But the matter is one which I think you should handle without reference to myself."

"You don't mean, if you know anything that might help, you won't give us a leg up?"

"I advised Mr. Nolan to be entirely frank with you, and you can be sure that my attitude will correspond."

"Did he seem willing to come or did you have to shove him along?"

"He agreed readily."

"Do you know where the young woman is now?"

"I am informed that she is staying at Jordans with Miss Patience Manly."

"The devil she is! I suppose I'm to understand by that that Miss Manly believes her tale?"

"That would be going too far. I was onto Miss Manly only a few minutes ago, and she told me that she has a most open mind."

"Then I don't understand—and besides there's the letter. I should have thought that—"

"The wording of the letter does not appear to have quite the same effects on the lay and the legal mind. But I need perhaps scarcely add that Miss Manly is not acting on my advice."

"I should say not. I suppose it's no use asking for your own opinion?"

"As to whether she's his wife or a blackmailer or perhaps both? Like Miss Manly, I am cultivating an open mind."

"I expect you've asked the secretarial bureau you had her from for any information upon their books?"

"Combridge has. It appears—as is reasonable—that they take students with very little regard for credentials, or none at all, especially if they pay in advance. Afterwards they recommend them according to their own experience of their conduct and abilities. That may be reasonable, but you'll see the opening it gives.

"I ought to add that what particulars she *did* give them coincide with her statements to me, except that she registered with them as an unmarried woman, which she now says she is not. But Combridge hadn't checked them when I heard from him last."

"It sounds to me as though Nolan will have to prosecute unless Combridge proves she's a fraud. That is, unless he breaks his engagement off."

"With some obvious reservations, I am disposed to agree. But that will be for you—or perhaps for Lady Eleanor—to decide."

"I suppose it hangs up the settlement for the time?"

"That again is for your decision—or Lady Eleanor's—but I cannot say that I should regard it as an unreasonable attitude."

"Thanks. I am asking Lady Eleanor to look in tomorrow. After that I shall know where I am."

Mr. Tilson hung up and summoned his secretary. He dictated a letter which he altered more than once before finally deciding the form in which he was content for it to go; but he was largely wasting his time, for Nolan saw Lady Eleanor that evening before the letter came to her hands.

They met, as they had arranged to do, at a reception given by Lady Eleanor's aunt, and Bruce lost no time in telling her about the trouble which confronted him.

"We won't dance," he said, "if you don't mind. Let's find a quiet corner somewhere. I've got something to tell you."

"Yes, of course. Over there looks about right, if we can reach it before it's taken."

She had assented readily, but with a slight contraction of her black brows. She had no premonition of what she was about to hear, but the difference between the lawyers over the proposed settlement was in her mind, and she hoped that Nolan wasn't going to refer to that again. After what she had said last night, surely he should be content to leave it to her?

Characteristically, she spoke at once, following her own thoughts: "I suppose you've seen Mr. Jellipot?"

"Yes, but it isn't that. At least, I mean—well, I'd better tell you just what's happened. I had a letter yesterday morning from a young woman whose name meant nothing to me, and whom—as far as I know—I've never met in my life. She asked me to send her money and threatened that she'd tell you something—she didn't say what— if I didn't.

"I took the letter to Mr. Jellipot, and—to cut the story short—it turns out that she's his own stenographer, who must have learnt about us from the correspondence which she'd been typing, and thought she could frighten me—blackmail is the proper word."

"It sounds like a matter for the police. But perhaps being Mr. Jellipot's clerk—though of course he won't keep her after that."

"I had put it in the hands of the police before we knew who she was. In fact, it was Chief Inspector Combridge who found it out. But the point is that when Mr. Jellipot talked to her, the young woman stuck to her tale and said she married me at a registry office a year or more ago."

"Of course, it's all lies?"

Lady Eleanor's tone was contemptuous rather than interroga- tory. It sounded an incredible tale and Nolan's frankness in telling her about it had a reassuring effect.

"Absolutely. Or she may be a bit queer in the head."

"Does she look like that?"

"I haven't seen her."

"But I thought you said—"

"Mr. Jellipot wouldn't let me."

"Why on earth not?"

"He didn't go into that. But he thought that, as she was in his employment, someone else had better act for me from the first. So I went to Cole and Tilson."

Eleanor looked surprised. "I shouldn't have thought you'd have gone to them. I didn't think you got on with Mr. Tilson."

"He doesn't like me. I know that. I suppose he thinks you're too good for me, as of course you are. But I thought he'd be the best one to handle this. And you'll know that nothing's been kept back from you."

"Aren't you taking it rather too seriously?"

"Perhaps I am. But she says I married her in another name, which might be a question of my word against hers. I've no doubt we shall get at the truth, but I don't know how much trouble it may mean, or how long it will take. I feel, however absurd it is, that it's got to be cleared up properly before we can be married, and we don't want anything to delay that."

"No, we don't want that." There was no doubt of the sincerity of her tone, or the reality of her love. Their eyes met, and it was plain that, had they been in a more solitary place, their lips would have done the same.

She added: "It was nice of you to take it to Mr. Tilson. I should think he could see that."

Bruce thought, if he had, he had concealed his feelings successfully, but he only said: "Well, he's got it in hand, and so have the police, so we can feel we're being looked after properly."

"Rather." She rose as though there were nothing more to be said, and next moment they had abandoned themselves to the sensuous rhythm of the dance. But there was a shadow now on both their minds—one that obtruded again and again and must be consciously cast aside.

Eleanor had had two suitors before, both of whom she had discarded somewhat abruptly, somewhat imperiously perhaps, but with cause enough. No one who knew the facts would be likely to question that.

She knew that she had beauty and wit sufficient to justify the confidence that she would be loved for herself—but she knew no less that it was her fortune that they had sought.

Now she had a lover of whom most women might be glad, were he rich or poor, and she had been resolved to transfer a substantial part of her wealth to him so absolutely that no subsequent idea of dependence might poison the ideality of their union. Mr. Tilson should have understood that and not been so grudging in what he gave. It was her money, not his! It had been her happiness that she sought to buy, and that was worth any amount of the money that seemed excessive to her.

She was confident in the reality of the affection of one whom she loved better than she had ever thought that she loved before, confident also in her ability to hold her lover by her own charms when all questions of money were put aside. At least, she saw that the full assurance of all she sought could be reached in no other way. If he should be financially dependent upon her, how could she ever be *quite* sure that he was not held by that golden chain? And she knew the jealousy of her own disposition well enough to be aware of how poisonous such a doubt would be. All that had been faced and settled, and put aside. But this was something—absurd, of course—but something of a kind of which she had never thought. If she should allow a doubt to enter her mind—but she would not. She put it firmly aside. And it came back, and had to be put even more firmly aside again. It would be disloyal—it would be *hateful*—to have such a doubt, to know afterwards that she had allowed it to enter her mind, after it had been exposed, as it was certain to be.

But she was glad that Charles had it in hand. She knew that she could depend on him. She had no fear that he would fail to discover the truth and to deal with it as the occasion would require. Her real fear, as she would have seen had she been honest with herself, to a degree which few women might reach, was that, if it were found to be true, she would be exposed as one who, for a third time, had accepted a worthless lover, to the extent of being almost drawn into a bigamous marriage. It would be an intolerable shame. But she did not think of it thus, because she did not allow herself to think of the possibility that it might be true. Loyalty and love might have been sufficient to exclude the doubt, but pride was a strong ally. So the doubt sat at the door of her mind, waiting to be let in.

There was no lack of warmth in her parting embrace that night. Rather, there was an added ardour. But neither of them alluded again to what was in both their minds.

Bruce was not unworried as he went back to his own rooms. Innocent or guilty, that would have been an unnatural complacency. But he felt that he had managed a difficult matter as well as could have been reasonably anticipated. Or even better than that.

CHAPTER XI.

LADY ELEANOR TAKES ADVICE

MR. TILSON was not surprised when Lady Eleanor walked into his office at about eleven o'clock next morning.

It was precisely what he had expected to happen. She was accustomed to call upon him without the formality of an appointment, and mid-morning was her usual time. He had no doubt that she would be on the warpath now, though less certain where her line of battle would lie.

But if doubts had made misery for her during a wakeful night, she was not going to show them to the lifelong friend who might have married her—did he know it? She sometimes wondered if, in her emphatic metaphor, he had had the pluck of a louse.

She showed no sign of any serious emotion as she toyed with one pulled-off glove, beyond the fact that her eyes, which always sparkled, were brighter than usual, and the colour of her cheeks, which she always had to tame rather than extend, a little more vividly red.

"Bruce," she said, "told me about it last night. I'm glad he did that; and I'm glad he brought it to you. It was the straightforward thing, and it couldn't have been pleasant for him to do. But I don't think that it's of any importance at all. Not beyond that it's got to be cleared up. I'm not going to have people say I've married a bigamist, and I don't want the marriage delayed because a blackmailer's running loose. But I can trust you to see to that."

"I hope you can. And I'm inclined to agree with you that it may not be a very serious matter—"

"Then I should say that settles it."

"That might be going too far."

"I don't think so. You don't like Bruce. If *you* say there's nothing in it—"

"I didn't quite say that. And whether I like Nolan or not has no relation to my judgement about a blackmailer's letter addressed to him."

"Anyway, you think that's what it is?"

"A blackmailer's letter? It speaks for itself. As a matter of fact, that proves nothing. All the people who get blackmailed are not innocent. In fact, such people rarely are."

"You can't mean—"

"I don't mean anything more than I say. But I've been having a talk with my partner, and I've had an idea from him to which he thinks we might have given more thought than we have. He says we may have been barking up the wrong tree because we've assumed that there are only two up which to bark.

"He means this: we've been assuming either that Nolan married and abandoned this girl, which isn't likely, especially in the way that she tells the tale, or else that she's an almost incredibly clumsy blackmailer of the worst type. But isn't there a third possibility? May she not be honestly mistaken about the identity of the man of whom, according to her own tale, she only caught a side glimpse as she came through one door and he passed out of another?"

"Mr. Cole thinks that? I shouldn't think he makes many mistakes."

"He merely suggested it as a possibility."

"But if that's how it was, she wouldn't persist in it after she'd found out her mistake."

"I don't know that they've met since."

"But I thought—"

"Mr. Jellipot wouldn't bring them together. One of his legal scruples, more likely than not."

"Then I think that ought to be done at once."

"I'm not sure that that would be the best way to proceed. You see, the letter remains. And in some ways it's no less serious if it were sent by mistake to the wrong man.

"I propose to prosecute the young woman so that they'll confront each other in court. If she says then that Nolan's the wrong man, it will be far better than getting a private admission, the genuineness of which might be doubted subsequently, and the magistrate could then deal with it in his own way."

"Won't it be making it all public, when it might be cleared up differently?"

"Yes-s, I see how you feel. But there are some arguments on the other side. In the first place, it mayn't mean as much publicity as you suppose. Nolan's name may not come out at all. The magistrate would almost certainly consent to deal with the matter so that it would not be published.

"Then you've got to consider that, if it be dropped without a decision being obtained, rumour might get about which would be increasingly hard to deal with as the years pass, and you wouldn't like that."

"No, I shouldn't like that."

"Beyond that, there's the point that the letter the woman wrote is an attempt at blackmail, whatever the facts may be—an attempt to extort money by threats—there's no getting away from that; and if Nolan should decline to prosecute, no one can make him, but it will have a bad sound."

Eleanor was silent for a long moment, her fingers toying with the loose glove. Then her face changed to a sudden smile. "I know you're right," she said. "I was just shirking a fence that I didn't like."

"I'm sure I am. I think you'd be sorry afterwards if it were dealt with in a different way. But," he added generously, "it's Nolan's decision, not mine. He's taking the right course and you've got to thank him for that."

There was gratitude as well as the intimacy of a long friendship in the glance she gave him as she replied: "It's like you to say that. Get it over quickly. That's all I ask."

She rose, shook hands, and went out in a buoyant way.

He had said no more than was true and than the occasion required. Nolan was dealing with it in the right way, as a guilty man might be unlikely to do. But he wished he were *quite* sure.

CHAPTER XII.

MR. NOLAN PROCEEDS

"WE HAVE advised Nolan," Mr. Tilson said, "that a prosecution is unavoidable."

Mr. Jellipot was not surprised. "It is what I had anticipated," he replied. "Am I to understand that your advice has been taken?"

"Yes. We are applying for a summons this afternoon."

"Then we should not have to wait long for the truth to come out. You have concluded that you have a good case?"

"It was a blackmailing letter. I do not see how any legal ingenuity can avoid that construction. But beyond that, the woman must almost certainly be entirely innocent, or a criminal of the worst type. It is hard to see any medium."

"That is the great difficulty of the case. May I conclude that the police will co-operate in suppressing Nolan's name and in publishing hers?"

"They will try to suppress his."

"It is the usual course. Yet it remains that it is unjust."

"I have never looked at it in that light." Mr. Tilson's face showed a sudden gravity as he added: "I might almost conclude that you are undertaking the young woman's defence?"

"Then you would conclude wrongly. I have not been asked to do so, and I should certainly have refused such a request. I seldom take criminal business, as you know, and it is particularly improbable that I should undertake the defence of one of whose innocence I was not convinced."

"So I have understood. May I take it that, in this instance, you have no such confidence?"

"Yes, you may. I regard it as a very puzzling affair. What I said would apply to such prosecutions generally. Both names should be published, or both suppressed."

"The police look at it from a different angle."

"That is because they are less concerned with equity than with obtaining convictions. Or perhaps," he added, with his usual scrupulosity, "I should say, with the suppression of crime."

Mr. Tilson did not pursue the subject further. He asked: "I suppose you don't know whether she's got anyone to act for her?"

"I have been told that there will be no difficulty about that."

"That means she's got someone with a full purse backing her up."

"Then I can assure you that it is not mine."

"I didn't suppose it was. I should say it's the gang behind her. It looks as though we may be in for a real fight."

"But perhaps you are assuming too much."

"I hope I am. The trouble is, in a case of this kind, that we don't know what we've got to meet till the defence opens up."

"If your client is frank with you, you should not be greatly embarrassed by that."

"Well, he says he knows nothing about her. If that's true, as I m supposed to believe, he can't say anything more. We can only wait to see what she will assert, and what evidence—perjured or otherwise—she can call to support it."

"She seems to me to have been specific and frank."

"To a point, yes. She might have said a lot more."

"We must agree there. Sooner or later, she'll have to say a lot more or you'll get a conviction. You may have plenty of time after the committal to check any allegations that she may make."

"Yes, I suppose we shall."

Mr. Tilson realised that Mr. Jellipot might know more than he was disposed to say. Well, he would not try to force an unwilling confidence. He got up to go.

CHAPTER XIII.

COMMITTAL

ELEANOR threw down the *Daily Telegraph* for the third time with an impatience she could not curb.

And yet she knew that it was unreasonable to expect the telephone to ring which she was so anxious to hear. It was barely noon. The hearing was to have commenced at ten-thirty.

She had been persuaded not to attend the magistrate's court, which she had been anxious to do, and Charles had promised to telephone her the result as soon as he got back to his office. He had warned her that the hearing might be prolonged, if the accused should elect to develop her defence. He had been too considerate to add that an abrupt termination might result from Nolan's being unable to sustain his denial, with all that it would imply. He had said truly that a committal was almost certain, and that, if Miss Westerham's lawyers should advise her to reserve her defence, the proceedings might not be long.

But it was only ten minutes later that she heard the expected sound, and then Charles's voice saying: "Go all right? Yes, of course. It was soon over, because they reserved their defence, and that meant a committal as a matter, of course."

"How soon will it be over now?"

"The hearing will be at the Old Bailey. It may not be more than three week from now, at a sanguine guess."

"And did she still profess to recognise Bruce?"

"They didn't give themselves away, even on that. But I ought to tell you that Nolan gave his evidence very well, and I think he was generally believed."

"I'm so glad. But I didn't really doubt how it would be."

"Well, I should just put it out of your mind. It's for us lawyers to deal with now. When Nolan's cleared it up, you'll like to think that you didn't doubt him at all."

She put the receiver back with the natural satisfaction that the report deserved, and yet with a vague undercurrent of hateful doubt. It was not what Charles had said. It was the faint doubt in the tone which had vexed her mind. Was he still unsure? And then she saw that she was being unjust to Bruce and unfair to Charles. She must allow for legal caution. And there was the fact that Bruce had come through the ordeal well. And how unpleasant it must have been! He would need comfort from her, which he should not miss.

And while she thought this, Charles Tilson had strolled into his partner's room to report the same event in a rather different way.

"She's got Fell and Unster defending her," he said. "I don't suppose they've taken a case like it in the last half century."

"No, nor longer than that. I suppose it means that Miss Manly has taken her up in earnest?"

"It looks that way. And they've briefed Bulmer."

Mr. Cole's eyebrows lifted, but he said nothing. There was a significance here which did not need to be put into words. He asked: "Of course she's got bail?"

"On a surety of £500. Miss Manly came forward at once."

There was really no more to be said. Fell and Unster were a prominent and highly respectable firm of solicitors, who had a large family practice among a law-abiding clientele. They might never have had any previous acquaintance with the criminal courts in the whole course of their century of practice. It could be safely assumed that it was on the insistence of Miss Patience Manly that they had reluctantly taken a distasteful case. And then they had briefed a barrister famous in criminal trials, who with equal certainty had never had a brief with their endorsement before—one who had the reputation of being unrivalled in getting the guilty out of the perils in which they stood.

As Miss Manly might be convinced of Edith Westerham's innocence, so it appeared even more definitely that Fell and Unster had assumed her guilt. And the course which Bulmer had taken had the same complexion. Would not an innocent, indignant woman have wished to go into the witness box at the first possible moment to tell the facts on which she relied?

But she had preferred to reserve her defence, as she was entitled to do. And this, if she were guilty, would have the tactical advantage that the assertions which must ultimately be made, should she stand her ground, would not be subject to the probing enquiries which would be possible during the interval between committal and trial.

"You'll have to wait," Mr. Cole remarked, "till the case comes on, to learn what she'll bring forward as evidence on her behalf, and if Nolan really knows nothing about her, there's not much you can do in the meantime. Except, of course, there's the witness to whatever marriage ceremony really took place, who's presumably still alive. You should be able to trace her, though it's doubtful what she may say, whether she's a truthful witness or not. How much would she remember now? And the other side may be on the same scent. And a good detective agency may find out enough about the girl in other ways to blast the whole case and settle the issue for you before you go into court."

"Yes, we can do that. Lady Eleanor says we're not to spare any expense. She means to have the thing turned inside out, at whatever cost and whatever the truth may be."

"And Nolan likes it being dealt with in that way?"

"So he says, and with a genuine sound."

"Probably because that's just what it is."

"Yes. I know I find it hard to be fair to him."

"Well, that's natural enough. But he may be a fortune-hunter who's getting not only the cash, but a girl it must be very easy to love, without having had a habit of marrying other women previously. That's mere logic, where prejudice may take you down the wrong road."

Charles could not dispute that, and anyway he had taken the case and was bound to do all that brains or money could to demonstrate his client's innocence, in a position which could not end with a verdict of acquittal, as is the possibility of most criminal prosecutions—for must there not be guilt in the witness box, if there should be innocence in the dock?

CHAPTER XIV.

DAY OF BATTLE

IT WAS 10:45 when Mr. Jellipot entered the crowded court and took a seat which Charles Tilson had kept for him, not without difficulty, on the solicitors' bench. It was not by choice but as a witness, that he was there, for it was a drama of doubtful justice, and inevitable resultant misery, which he would have preferred to avoid.

He knew already that the enquiries which had been made concerning Edith Westerham had been without decisive results. It was her maiden name. She had certainly married *someone* who had given the name of Henry Lingfield at the place and on the date that she alleged. One witness of that marriage was dead, and the other could not be traced. Miss Lucille Belloes had left her address two days after the letter had been written. At the service flatlet she rented, she had said that she was going on a holiday, and had paid a week's rent in lieu of notice. At the export merchant's office where she was employed, she had simply failed to appear, leaving them to think what they would.

It was an almost certain conclusion that this sudden disappearance was connected with the event which was now before the court. It was a natural presumption that she had gone away as the result of an approach by one or other of the protagonists in the case. How else should she have heard of it at all? But if so, which had it been and why?

There had been intensive efforts to trace her, in which both sides had shown real or simulated eagerness. On the one side, Mr. Jellipot's knowledge of the character of the prosecuting solicitor assured him that they had been genuine. Private detectives had been employed. The assistance of the police had been sought. Finally, a week ago, a reward of £100 had been offered for the address of the missing woman. That would have been paid from Lady Eleanor's purse.

But all efforts had been in vain. Or would she appear with dramatic effect at the last moment, to give evidence which would be ruin to Bruce Nolan, or close prison gates on his false accuser?

It had been discovered that after the wedding the bridal pair had gone to Ireland, stayed for two nights at a Dublin hotel (where they were not remembered at all), and then gone onto Killarney, where they had put up at a cottage with a Mr. and Mrs. O'Leary, who remembered them—almost well enough, but not quite.

These addresses had been given to him by Mrs. Lingfield (which seemed to be the least disputable name to use) when she had made her first explanation. After some debate of conscience, he had decided that it was his duty to pass them onto the prosecution, and it was to be observed in her favour that they had been true.

Mr. Tilson had sent one of his own office staff to Killarney, thinking that if the O'Learys were prepared to say definitely that Bruce Nolan was not the man, it would be decisive for the prosecution; and, should there be an opposite result, it was not a conviction, it was the truth that it was essential for Lady Eleanor, whom he was subconsciously disposed to regard as his real client, to have.

But the result had been unsatisfactory. Shown photographs of Edith, both the O'Learys had identified her with confidence. But when shown that of Nolan, Mrs. O'Leary had said at first that it was the man, but when she had understood that she might be required to swear to this in a London Court, she became vaguer. She said that, after all, she was not that sure.

Her husband had thought it was very like, but that their visitor had had darker hair. Till he could see the man himself, he would prefer not to say more than that.

Mr. Tilson had debated the advisability of bringing over these witnesses with his partner, with his client, with Lady Eleanor, and in his own mind, and had finally decided that it was a risk he ought not to take.

Suppose (and they would probably support each other) they should make an error of identification?

It was not his business to prove a negative. Let the other side call them, if they had the courage, and the advantage of cross-examination would then be his.

Mr. Gilchrist-Walker, whom he had briefed, a sound man, and one to choose in a case in which it was of first importance that the truth should be reached, also hesitated, but finally took the same view. It was a risk which in Mr. Nolan's interest he ought not to advise.

Apart from that, the O'Leary's could have said no more than that the young couple had stayed with them for over three weeks, seeming very happy together, but during the fourth the man had left suddenly without explanation, which the girl had subsequently attempted to give, though in a state of distress she could not entirely conceal. She had left two days later, paying the final bill.

Enquiries at the address where she had told Mr. Jellipot she had left a baby had also confirmed her story. From there she had been traced backward to the Maternity Home where it had been born, and forward to the room she had taken in Ashfield Terrace, and her course of study at the Secretarial Training College from which she had entered Mr. Jellipot's office.

It could be observed that her tale was confirmed in every detail, except that which it was essential for her to prove, and, as to that, what could be done but to await the evidence she would put forward? And how, if it should be false, could anyone tell what it would be likely to be?

But, as to that, Mr. Gilchrist-Walker said that there was no cause for disquiet. He could not recall a case where a blackmailer had appeared to succeed in putting forward a lying tale. *Magna est veritas*—they could rely on that. It was not his part to suggest a doubt of whether truth would be helpful to them.

Now Mr. Jellipot looked at Bruce—Mr. X, as he had become for the following hours—sitting beside Lady Eleanor, with a gravity suitable to the occasion, but yet with a quiet confidence which it was reassuring to see.

He saw the girl make a smiling remark, as though to show that she was not concerned with the issue, but only that her lover should have no cause to question her faith in him. He saw her hand linger for a moment in a caressing motion over the one that rested beside it. There could be no doubt of what her feelings were.

He saw Miss Patience Manly also; she had taken a seat as near the dock as was possible, the court being arranged as it was, and he remembered that she had told him only three nights before that she was certain that she was giving shelter to a wronged and innocent girl.

He looked next at a rather nondescript jury and wondered whether, when they should be called upon for a verdict, the case would have become clearer than it now was. Well, it was a reasonable anticipation.

He rose mechanically with those around him as Mr. Justice Yoxall entered the court.

CHAPTER XV.

THE CASE FOR THE PROSECUTION

MR. JUSTICE YOXALL was a sound judge, patient, watchful, courteous to all, and with a reputation for inscrutability, so that the most observant might fail to guess where his sympathies lay, or what his judgement would be likely to be. He had a name also for leniency rather than severity in summing-up, and his sentences were seldom harsh, unless he had exceptional meanness or brutality with which to deal. But this could not be a case for mercy (unless in regard to penalty, if a conviction should be obtained); it could not be a question of giving the accused the benefit of the doubt. The truth must be sought and found, or injustice must necessarily be the result.

Now he listened to Mr. Gilchrist-Walker's statement of his client's case, fairly, moderately, very briefly given. It was a presentation which he approved. Without appearing to do so, he studied the girl in the dock. She was pale and quiet. He did not regard her as of a criminal type. But he could recall instances of attractive, innocent-looking young women of ready mendacities who had been convicted, beyond shadow of doubt, of repulsive crimes. He must regard all with an open mind.

He turned his attention to the prosecutor, who had now entered the witness box.

With calm assurance, "Mr. X" identified the letter which he had received. It was passed up to the judge, who read it. Now the witness went onto describe his subsequent actions, which appeared to be those of an innocent man.

The examination continued: "Are you in fact married to the writer of that letter?"

"No, certainly not."

"Look at her now. Do you know her?"

Bruce looked at the girl in the dock. The silent watchful court saw that their eyes met. In those of the man there was blank negation. In those that met his, there was an aspect of cold contempt. (What good actresses some women are!)

"No," he said. "I do not know her at all."

"Are you married?"

"No."

"Were you ever?"

"No, never."

"But you were, and are, engaged to the lady to whom allusion is made in the last sentence of the letter?"

"Yes, I am glad to say that I am."

"I think that is all that I need to ask."

Mr. Gilchrist-Walker sat down, and Mr. Bulmer rose to cross-examine.

"On the 4th of May last," he asked, "the day on which this letter was written, you called at the offices of your solicitor, Mr. Jellipot?"

"Yes."

"I want you to cast your mind back to the moment of leaving. I believe that, on leaving the inner room, you had to pass through an outer office. Did you pause there or have occasion to observe its occupants?"

"No, why should I? I went straight out."

"So I supposed. Did you observe anyone, man or woman, coming out of another door?"

"No, I just went out, without looking round at all."

"So that any glimpse that anyone may have caught of you, on entering that room by another door, must have been momentary?"

Bruce hesitated a moment, being puzzled as to where this unexpected examination might lead, but he could see no trap, and gave a natural and quite truthful reply: "Yes, I should think it would."

And then he found that there was no trap, nor were there to be any more questions at all. Mr. Bulmer sat down, as one who had learnt all that he wished to know.

Eleanor thought: "It's all over, really. It's just what Mr. Cole suggested. They're going to say she made a mistake."

Mr. Justice Yoxall thought much the same, though with a more critical mind.

Mr. Truscott, Fell and Unster's managing clerk, who was there to assist counsel, felt that they had been let down, but none of them was entirely right, and Mr. Truscott was not entirely fair.

He had had friction with Mr. Bulmer more than once during the past fortnight.

The learned counsel thought that it was his first duty to get an acquittal. If a line of defence were proposed which he thought likely to fail in securing that, it was of little interest to him to be told that it was the truth.

"Get that witness to the marriage," he had said, "and get her support, and we may have something we can get our teeth into. We might then have a fighting chance. I can't say that till I know what she'll be prepared to swear and what explanation she'll give for clearing out, but we may have a chance.

"But without her—what's the use of its being true if it can't be proved? She'll go to Holloway just the same, and we shall have let her down. There's only one sensible thing to say: that she made a mistake. She hasn't seen the man since that day, and when she gets a good look at him in court she sees that she's wrong, and she has the honesty to say so at once. She may even get some sympathy if she does that. Does she wear glasses? Well, anyway, her sight's not very good. Nobody's is.

"It's your part to prepare a decent defence, and it's mine to shove it down the jury's throats. But just to assert what you can't prove, when you've got to get over a letter that's blackmail beyond dispute, is just to make conviction *certain*, and the penalty about ten times more than it would otherwise be."

Faced by the fact that the defendant would not accept this advice, and that Mr. Truscott, who had come near to sharing Miss Manly's confidence in his client's innocence, supported her view that she could not say what she did not believe, he had reluctantly accepted instructions he did not like. But he still wished to hold open the door of retreat to the last possible second. For if he could do no more than to make the judge believe that she had first written the letter in honest mistake, and then been too stubborn to admit her error, she would still have written it in good faith, and it might have weight, however limited, when the time for sentence should come.

Beyond that, he did not see any good purpose in challenging the witness to repeat the denials that he had made. It might only increase their emphasis and the impression that would make on the jury. And what material had he on which a damaging cross-examination could have been based?

No, it would be better to let him go. So Bruce stepped down, and Mr. Jellipot entered the box.

The new witness, having given his evidence with clearness and brevity, including a quietly convincing word as to Miss Westerham's satisfactory conduct while in his employment, was subject to a somewhat long cross-examination, at the end of which Mr. Truscott looked better pleased.

"You have said that Miss Westerham—as she was known to you—had been in your employment for several months before this incident occurred, and that her conduct in that confidential position had been satisfactory. Is it reasonable to conclude that you had never had reason to think that she had made use of confidential information before?"

"Obviously not, or I should not have kept her on."

"And there must have been previous occasions when she might have taken advantage of what she knew more or less in the same way?"

Mr. Jellipot paused before he replied, and then answered carefully: "Yes, at least four—in different ways and degrees."

"And if we assume the facts to be as she afterwards told you, her reaction was not unnatural?"

"It was entirely wrong. She should have reported her suspicion to me."

"That was not precisely what I asked. You would hardly expect a girl in that position to act with the judgment and discretion of a practising solicitor?"

"No."

"And when she did give you her explanation, you took it seriously? You did not act towards her as you would have done had you regarded it as a blackmailer's lie?"

Mr. Jellipot again paused before answering. Then he said, with slow deliberation: "When she first told her tale, I had an impression of truth and sincerity."

"Which you still have?"

"I will not go beyond what I have said. I regard it as a most puzzling case."

The judge looked as though he were on the point of asking a further question, and then made a slight motion of his hand, as though putting the purpose aside.

Mr. Truscott thought correctly that the first doubt of where the truth might be had disturbed the minds of those who heard.

Eleanor wondered whether Mr. Jellipot had intended to give support to the idea that a genuine error might have been made. But in fact he had had no thought beyond being most exactly truthful on a matter which was unsolved in his own mind.

He returned to his place to observe a slow-ticking clock on the wall the hands of which gave the time as eleven-fifty. It had taken scarcely an hour for the prosecution to make its case.

CHAPTER XVI.

MRS. LINGFIELD IN THE WITNESS BOX

MR. BULMER addressed his own witness in his quietest, most conversational tone.

"You do not deny writing the letter which is the basis of the charge which has been brought against you?"

"Oh, no, I wrote it. I meant every word."

"Please do not go beyond answering my questions. At that time you had no doubt that it was addressed to a man whom you had married—a Mr. Lingfield?"

"None at all."

"Though you had only caught a glimpse of him as he had gone out through the door?"

"I saw him quite plainly. You don't forget a man you've been married to for nearly a month."

"*If* you see him plainly, that may be true. At any rate, the letter was written in that belief. Did you know that the demand you made could be construed as a legal offence?"

"No, it seemed reasonable to me. We've got a child, though I daresay he didn't know that. Why shouldn't he do something for it?"

"That is to say, that it seemed reasonable to you, believing him to be the father of your child, to ask him for an annual allowance, or else go to the wealthy woman he was proposing to marry and lay your position before her?"

"Yes, I saw nothing wrong in that. I don't now."

Mr. Bulmer made an impressive pause. He was not entirely pleased with the answers he was receiving, but he had already recognised that he was not dealing with a client who would follow with obedient feet a path which he might indicate. And the bold assertions that she was making might rouse assent in at least some of the twelve on whom her freedom must ultimately depend.

Beyond that, might not her stubborn assumption that the prosecutor was the man she married make a stronger impression on some minds than a simple assertion would be likely to do? And as to the possibility that she might have made a mistake of recognition, had he not in his opening questions shown her the path which she might even yet have the sense to take?

He tried once again. "So it is the case that you have not seen the man whom you recognised as your husband from the moment of that instantaneous glimpse until today?"

"Yes, it is. But if you're trying to get me to say that I made a mistake, it's no use at all. The man who married me at the Registry Office and deserted me in Ireland is sitting behind you now, only two seats away."

Mr. Bulmer recognised defeat.

Let Gilchrist-Walker try what he could do. Perhaps he might find it as difficult in an opposite way.

So she observed, without particular interest, that one counsel sat down and another rose, and that questions now came from a different mouth.

"Now, Mrs. Lingfield," he began, in no bullying manner, for he was not of that type, but in a voice that suggested that after needless time-wasting they were coming to facts at last, "we understand that you were married at Marylebone Registry Office on June 22nd, 1927 to a gentleman whom you knew as Henry Lingfield. Where did you go after the ceremony?"

"We went to Dublin."

"And then?"

"To a cottage in Killarney."

"How long did you stay there?"

"Between three and four weeks."

"Then you must both have become well known to the people there?"

"I don't see why we should."

"Your husband was a fine-looking Englishman?"

"You can see what he is."

"I am asking you."

"Yes. That was why I was such a fool."

"The people with whom you stayed and the neighbours—is any of them here now?"

"You should know best. I heard that you were afraid to bring them."

"You shouldn't believe everything that you hear. It was not our business to do so. Anyway, you are not producing anyone from Killarney who could identify your husband?"

Mr. Bulmer rose quickly. As he did so, he said in a low whisper: "You got out of that rather well." Then he said: "I must object. The witness cannot be required to disclose how she will conduct her defence."

Mr. Gilchrist-Walker gave way. He asked: "And after you left Killarney?"

"You mean where did I go? He had walked out on me. I went to Lynmouth."

"You just stayed there doing nothing?"

"More or less. I tried to find him, of course. I just stayed there till the baby came."

"Then your husband didn't leave you penniless?"

"He would have done if he could. He took more than three hundred pounds."

"And of course you informed the police?"

"No, I didn't want any fuss about it."

"How can you say that he left you purposely? That he didn't intend to come back? I should have thought that it would have been a most natural thing to have enlisted the help of the police."

"Because he told me."

"You mean you quarrelled and he told you he was leaving you?"

"We didn't quarrel. He said it like a joke. He said: 'I'm going out for some cigarettes. Perhaps you'll never see me again.' And then, as the time passed, I understood and looked for his suitcase, and it was gone."

"And you never saw him again?"

"I can see him sitting there now."

"Mrs. Lingfield, even now, wouldn't it be better to admit you made a mistake?"

"I haven't made any. I wouldn't tell that lie if I knew it would get me out of this, and nothing else would. Not though I were to be in prison for all my life."

With a slight gesture of his hand, as of one who left folly to its natural fate, counsel sat down.

Mr. Jellipot, who had watched the witness closely, admitted an inclination to credit her tale, but was not fully convinced. Her manner had become different from when she had been his trusted stenographer, different from when she had first told this improbable tale to him—almost sullen, bitter, even aggressive. Perhaps it was natural enough, if she were telling a true tale which was rejected by all who heard it.

But he observed also that her last answers had revealed a motive, both for the marriage and the desertion, which had come out more convincingly in cross-examination than if it had been an assertion of the defence. She had been married by an unscrupulous fortune-hunter, and that—without the adjective—was an expression which could be applied to Nolan suitably enough. He looked, as the thought came, at a man who sat with an aspect of quiet ease beside a girl whose confidence in him was demonstrated by her presence there. Could anyone have heard that account of his own infamy and be as poised, as unconcerned, as Nolan was now?

Mr. Justice Yoxall, half listening to the speeches of counsel, which were for the jury rather than him, pondered his summing-up and had much the same doubt. He observed also a feature of the case which had not been mentioned on either side: the improbability that the errant husband should have happened to come to the office of the solicitor by whom the girl had been employed, when engaged in another enterprise of the same kind. He knew that it was not incredible. Such things do occur. But it was still a weight in a doubtful scale.

He saw clearly that, had it been merely a question of the girl's guilt or innocence, the evidence was such that it would have been his inclination, perhaps his duty, to sum up in such a way that no jury would be likely to convict. But it was less simple than that. To acquit her was to call the prosecutor a fraudulent scoundrel and a prospective bigamist, which could not be lightly done.

Well, it was for the jury to say! He commenced a summing-up of such scrupulous impartiality that even the experienced lawyers who heard him were left in doubt of where his own judgment lay. But of the legal impropriety of the letter itself he made it clear that there could be no doubt at all.

In the jury room there must have been dissension or the same doubt, for it was over two hours before their verdict was delivered, and then it was of an illogical kind: *Guilty, but with a strong recommendation for mercy.*

What was the sense in that? If she were guilty, she was a blackmailer who had persisted stubbornly in a false accusation of the worst kind. Surely there should be no exceptional mercy for her!

Appearing not to notice this anomaly and with equal obliviousness of the exclamation of dismay which came from the dock, Mr. Justice Yoxall passed a sentence of nine months' imprisonment, which certainly did not err on the side of severity.

As the wardress touched the prisoner's arm to lead her away, Miss Patience Manly rose from her seat. "My lord," she asked, "may I have a word with Mrs. Lingfield before she is taken away?"

It was a tribute to the personality of the speaker that the judge showed no consciousness of the irregularity of this approach. He asked courteously: "You are a relative?"

"No, my lord, a friend. But I want her to know that this case will not be dropped till we reach the truth."

Mr. Justice Yoxall did not look pleased. The court became alert in expectation of his rebuke. But when he spoke it was only to say coldly: "Then I think she will already have heard what you have to say."

CHAPTER XVII.

EPISODES

LADY ELEANOR called on her solicitor.

"Charles," she said, "now that this bother is out of the way, I want you to complete the settlement as soon as possible; We are arranging the marriage for Monday, the 23rd."

Mr. Tilson did not look pleased. He began to ask: "Do you think—?" And checked the words which were best unsaid. Was it reasonable, was it fair to Nolan, to suggest that the engagement should be broken because of an accusation which had led to the imprisonment of the one who made it? Was he unbiased in his own judgment?

"Everything is practically complete," he said. "We will get in touch with Mr. Jellipot at once."

She showed consciousness of much which was left unsaid when she answered: "Thank you, Charles. I knew you'd see it in the right way."

Miss Manly met Mr. Jellipot for dinner at the usual place. She said: "I want you to do something for me, want you to go on hunting that Belloes woman. If she'd been found before this, I don't suppose Edith would be in jail now."

"Possibly not," he replied, "or it might have been two years instead of the short sentence she got. What do you suppose the woman's evidence would have been?"

"I think she must have been afraid that she'd be required to give evidence about the marriage, and she daren't do it because someone's got a hold over her. That seems the most likely theory to me."

"It is a possible explanation. But there is a preliminary question of how she could have learnt so quickly that the question had arisen."

"Yes. If we could find out that, I suppose there wouldn't be much left that we shouldn't know."

He had a different theory in his mind from that which had been suggested but it was best unspoken, even to her, being without evidence in its support and of a most libellous kind.

* * * * * * *

Mr. Wilton, one of the rulers of England, whose name was not known to a hundred people outside his immediate circle, sat in his softly-carpeted room (the thickness of his carpet being the mark of rank which was recognised throughout the bureaucracy to which he belonged), and considered a letter on the Lingfield case which had been passed upward to him. Mr. Wilton was quite used to receiving letters from members of the general public advising or even informing the Home Office officials of their duties; usually these were written in hysterical or abusive terms, but this letter seemed singularly business-like.

It said:

> It is only right that you should know that active enquiries are being made to establish the innocence of Edith Lingfield, in which the cooperation of the Metropolitan police would be welcome. Would it not be well for the Home Office to have the credit of doing justice, seeing that the discredit of injustice is so near to its door?

It bore the signature of Patience Manly. Mr. Jellipot, who had been asked to write it but had declined, would have worded it differently, but its meaning would have been the same. (Mr. Truscott had also been invited to send it, but had excused himself for more diffident reasons.)

After an interval for reflection, Mr. Wilton picked up one of his telephones. He asked: "Who was the judge in the trial of a recent convict, Edith Lingfield? Yoxall? Get me through to him now, if he's out of court."

In less than three minutes, the voice of Mr. Justice Yoxall, who had been engaged upon an excellent lunch, could be heard on another line.

He said: "Yes, it was quite a proper conviction. Blackmailing letter, and no defence beyond unsupported assertions by the prisoner. But I don't go beyond that. I wasn't satisfied that the truth came out. Nor were the jury. Illogical recommendation to mercy. Nine months. Must have served three weeks or a bit more. Scotland

Yard? Yes, by all means. And let whoever they put onto it have a word with me."

* * * * * * *

Lady Eleanor, now three days married, and having found a lover who gave her joy, picked up the letters which the waiter had laid beside her. She was at the hotel breakfast table, where Bruce might join her at any moment. She recognised a familiar envelope, one from her own bank, and slit it automatically. Next moment, as she looked at the letter which it contained, she saw that it was not for her, and put it back.

She handed it to Bruce, as he sat down beside her. "I slit this by mistake," she said. "It's for you."

"What does it matter?" he answered carelessly, putting it into his pocket without looking at its contents.

His wife said nothing, but in the brief moment before she had realised that it was not for her, its single sentence had reached her mind: "We are writing to advise you that, after cashing a cheque for £1,000 today, your account is overdrawn £47 3s. 2d., which will doubtless have your early attention."

It had been a few days before the marriage that £1,000, the first instalment of her settlement upon him, had been transferred to Bruce's credit at her own bank. She knew that he had drawn cheques upon it for from £40 to £50, mainly for gifts to her. Why had he now withdrawn, or transferred, the whole amount, without even allowing for these minor payments? She knew that he was not rich, but he had always seemed to be sufficiently supplied for current needs. Well, there might be a simple explanation of that, and anyhow it would be unmannerly to enquire into what had been discovered in such a way.

CHAPTER XVIII.

MRS. BRUCE NOLAN CALLS

MR. JELLIPOT looked up in some surprise as his managing clerk entered the room. "Newman," he said mildly, "I did ask that I should not be disturbed for the next hour."

"Yes, sir. But a lady has called to see you, giving the name of Mrs. Bruce Nolan, and I thought you would not wish me to send her away, or perhaps to discuss it with you over the phone."

"You mean it is not Lady Eleanor?"

"I haven't seen her, but I should say certainly not."

"You have been as discreet as usual. Did she confide anything further to you?"

"She said that she had called on a matter which she could discuss only with you."

"Very well, you must show her in."

A minute later, a rather tall, angular, plain-featured woman entered the room. She carried a small but heavy rectangular parcel, which she continued to hold firmly on her lap with both hands after she had subsided into the comfort of the low chair at the side of the solicitor's table.

Showing no sign of surprise or doubt, Mr. Jellipot enquired: "You are Mrs. Bruce Nolan?"

"Yes. I think I'm first on the list."

"And you have an urgent matter on which to see me?"

"I've come about the money. It's getting too hot to hold."

As she spoke, she began to unwrap the parcel, disclosing a thick wad of one-pound notes, which were evidently in the original condition in which they had been received from the bank; a thick, solid, square-cornered block.

"I am afraid it is a matter of which I know nothing."

"You're Bruce's solicitor? That's what I was told."

"I have acted for Mr. Nolan on some occasions."

68

"Well, I didn't want to risk the post, or to call where there might be more of a row than I'd want to have, so I thought I'd better bring it to you and have a proper receipt."

"I'm afraid I couldn't accept such a responsibility, if at all, without knowing far more than I do now."

"Well, that's fair enough. It's like this. I married Bruce about ten years ago. I'd had a legacy of a thousand dollars from an aunt in Denver, and he saw a letter which made him think it was a hundred times that amount—there were two noughts at the end for the cents. You know how they write it. It is confusing if you don't notice the comma or understand what it means.

"He didn't let on that he'd seen the letter, and only found out the truth after we were married. He wouldn't believe it at first, but after that there was hell's own row. I knew him by then for the slimy hound that he is, and when he tried bullying, I picked up a carving knife, and told him he'd have it between the ribs if he ever came near me again."

"It is possible to appreciate how you felt. But, so far as you know, it was a legal marriage?"

"I don't think there's much doubt about that."

"May I conclude that you resumed your maiden name? And is it too rash to guess that it is Lucille Belloes?"

"You're right in one. I saw he'd only married me to get hold of something I hadn't got. He'd had most of what little there was by then—and I only wanted to make sure that he'd never put his hands on me again."

"But I conclude that you have seen him at a more recent date than you have yet mentioned?"

"Yes. He came and gave me fifty pounds, which wasn't much for what he asked me to do, but he said he'd find a thousand in three months and that much more every year afterwards, if I'd clear out and keep hidden, so that I couldn't be found."

"Did he give you any reason for this very liberal offer?"

"Yes, he said he'd got the chance of a rich marriage so long as they didn't get hold of me."

"You thought it right to be a party to that?"

"Well, what harm would there have been? It puts him out of circulation, if it lasts, and he'll be no more nuisance to other girls. Men don't look at questions like that in a practical way."

"Then why are you bringing this money to me?"

"I told you that. It's getting too hot to hold. I didn't mind chucking up everything if I got well enough paid for it, and I don't mind who he marries so long as it keeps him away from me, but when I find the police smelling around, and as close to me as they are now—well, it's a bit too thick. It's not I who's the bigamist, and I don't want any truck with them."

"Yes. I can understand your objection. Especially if you were one of the witnesses at a subsequent marriage to Miss Westerham?"

"So you know that? I suppose that's what they're trying to put on me now? If that tricky dog—!"

Her voice failed, as it seemed that, perhaps for the first time, she realised the full gravity of her position. Her face flushed with anger and bitter hatred of the man of whom she was probably the legal wife.

Meanwhile, Mr. Jellipot was analysing the position and its legal consequences with his habitual leisurely thoroughness. He said: "It is, I should suppose, most unusual for a bigamist to ask his wife to witness the second ceremony in her maiden name. May I ask what led you to do this?"

"Well, he gave me twenty pounds, and I was wanting a new dress at the time, and of course it looked as though I were getting him off my hands, so that I could go my own way. I haven't done anything serious, have I? Not if I give back the money now."

"You certainly acted in a way that the law would not approve. But now serious it may be for you may partly depend upon the degree to which you assist the cause of justice now."

Actually, she had asked something to which he was not prepared to give an instant reply. It appeared probable that she had succeeded in one of the most difficult of human enterprises—committing an absolutely unprecedented, original crime. He could not even decide without reflection whether or how far it could be dealt with by laws which had not contemplated its commission.

But the idea of "assisting justice" did not appear to rouse enthusiasm, even as a method of self-protection. She said in a tone of sulky obstinacy: "I'd rather give you back the money and have nothing more to do with it. It's not my affair."

"It is a point of view with which there might be no general agreement. And in any case I could not undertake the custody of money which has almost certainly been obtained from Lady Eleanor Cresswell by the basest fraud.

"My advice to you is not to return it to Mr. Nolan, but to take it to Lady Eleanor, to whom it rightly belongs, with a frank statement of the facts you have told to me. And if I have your assurance that you will do that, I may decide to explain the position in the meantime to her solicitors, who may inform her of it at their discretion, so that she may be prepared for what you will say."

"I shouldn't like to do that."

"It is a matter for you to decide. But if you dislike the idea of a confined life, it is a course which you would be prudent to take."

The woman sat silent for some moments, with the expression of sulky obstinacy still on her face, but when she spoke, she said: "I'll go to see her tomorrow morning. You'd better let me have her address, and say I shall be there at twelve. It's about what he deserves, and I should say that what you call a confined life is what's coming to him."

"It is a point on which I am disposed to agree."

So perhaps most people would, but those who foretell the future are seldom right.

CHAPTER XIX.

A CONFERENCE BETWEEN LAWYERS

FOR some time after Mrs. Nolan had left, Mr. Jellipot sat in silent thought, seeing tragedy ahead which he must be active to introduce, though he could not foretell what its end would be. Then he picked up the telephone. "Get me through to the Home Office," he said. "I wish to speak to Mr. Wilton on a matter of particular urgency."

He was connected almost immediately. "Mr Wilton's secretary speaking. That is Mr. Jellipot? One moment." Then he heard Mr. Wilton's voice "That you, Jellipot? Something about the Lingfield case, I suppose?"

"Yes. I have listened to a tale of extraordinary character in the last hour, but I have no doubt of its truth in some essential particulars. I conclude that Nolan will be under arrest within the next forty-eight hours."

"I can't say I'm surprised. The C.I.D. are on a hot scent, but you seem to have been a bit quicker than they. Does it let the girl out?"

"Yes, completely. The sooner you set her free and let her know that her job's waiting for her here, if she cares to come back, the less her claim for compensation will be."

"I don't know about that yet. When a jury—"

"Well, we needn't discuss that now. And it will be Fell and Unster's affair rather than mine. But you might like to let her know that she's never been Nolan's wife. I should regard it as a reasonable proposition," he concluded, relapsing into his more normal and leisurely manner, "that it is information which any reasonable woman would be delighted to have."

"Yes? But are reasonable women easy to find? And there must be two sides to that. There's the child. But it shows that you and Carver have been on the same scent, though you've got there first."

Mr. Jellipot heard this compliment with a punctilious consciousness that he was being praised for something which he had not done. "I think," he said, "you may be giving me credit I have not earned. I should say that Carver has flushed the game, and that it ran into my office as the result, expecting a shelter it did not get."

He went on to give a full account of the interview which had just terminated. But when he rang off at last, with the assurance that Edith Westerham's release would not be delayed, he had to turn his mind to a conversation it would be less pleasant to have. Yet it was one which must not be shirked. He gave instructions that he should be put through to Cole and Tilson, and was soon speaking to the junior partner.

"I have learnt something," he said, "this afternoon which is unsuitable for communication by telephone, and which in Lady Eleanor's interest you should know at once. Shall I come round to you?"

"No, if it's like that, I ought to come over to you. Anything about Nolan? Nothing really bad?"

"Yes. It depends upon how you look at it, whether you call it bad. But I'd better not say any more."

"I'll come at once."

Fifteen minutes later, Charles Tilson arrived. He came in with more evidence of suppressed excitement than a solicitor will commonly show even concerning the affairs of his most valued client, but he heard the vital fact, as Mr. Jellipot put it in one sentence of lucid brevity, without comment; and then listened quietly to a more leisurely and detailed statement with fluctuating feelings, as sympathy for the woman he loved, satisfaction in the coming downfall of a man he had cause to hate, realisation of what it might ultimately mean in happiness both for Eleanor and himself, became dominant in his mind. But with a lawyer's instinct for the essential fact, he saw the possibility that Eleanor might be freed from what must surely become to her a loathsome union without the unpleasantness of instituting legal proceedings, and—was it not also possible?—without being brought into public notice at all.

He said: "I suppose you will advise Miss Westerham to prosecute now?"

"So I might, if I should consider it my place to advise her at all. But I suppose Fell and Unster will decide that."

"Well, I suppose they'll soon hear how the land lies. We shall have to ask them what they intend to do."

"Yes, but if, as I am disposed to conclude, you are hoping that Lady Eleanor may escape the publicity which such proceedings entail, I must suggest that it will be impossible, on more grounds than one. His bribery of his wife and the source from which the money certainly came will inevitably lead to a full disclosure. You will do her a poor service if you do not advise her to adjust her mind to an ordeal which must be repugnant, but will soon be over, and in which she will have very general sympathy."

"Yes, but I don't think sympathy's what she'll enjoy. I think I'd better let her know the facts before that woman can get to her tomorrow, and that'll be best done at my own office. I'll ask her to see me on a matter of urgency not later than ten-fifteen."

"I don't think," Mr. Jellipot answered with decision, "that you can do better than that."

CHAPTER XX.

LADY ELEANOR LEARNS THE TRUTH

LADY ELEANOR entered her solicitor's office in good spirits, though with some curiosity as to what could have occasioned the hurried appointment at so early an hour.

She had had her first quarrel with Bruce on the previous night, on the small matter of his interference with a servant in a way which she felt to be derogatory to her own authority, which had been followed by apology and reconciliation in the early morning hours. Bruce had, she acknowledged to herself, been even more tenderly apologetic and contrite than the occasion had fairly required, and she was correspondingly tender in her own feelings to him. Her caution in the choice of one who would share her life had been justified by its results. She recognised that she was a very fortunate woman.

She said: "Hullo, Charles! What's the idea of bringing me here before I've had time to yawn?" in so cheerful a voice that he recognised that she had no faintest premonition of that which she was about to hear. But next moment she showed, in a sudden sobriety, that she had become aware of the gravity of the eyes which looked into hers.

He said: "I'm afraid what I've got to tell you won't be pleasant to hear. It's about Bruce."

"You don't mean to tell me that you've raked up something more about him and brought me here at this hour for nothing better than that?"

Her eyes were bright with a resentment which was half anger and half surprise, and he may have come to the point more abruptly in consequence. "The fact is that he did go through a marriage ceremony with Miss Westerham. The living witness has turned up. She says that she was his first wife."

Eleanor stared at this concise summary of surprising fact and could be excused if it sounded unconvincing to her. She said: "You haven't really brought me here to be told such nonsense as that."

"I'm afraid it's not nonsense at all. Nolan has just given her a thousand pounds to keep quiet and out of the way. Mr. Jellipot's actually seen the cash."

"Well, I don't believe a word of it. It sounds utter rot. It must be something that the friends of that girl have faked up to get her out of—" And then her voice died away, and the scorn in her eyes was changed to a startled fear, for she remembered the letter from the bank which had not been addressed to her.

He saw that her defence was weakened and followed up his advantage swiftly. "The woman is coming to see you this morning to tell you the whole tale. I thought you might prefer to hear it from me."

She controlled herself by a strong effort. She sat down, for she had been standing till now. She said: "I'm not promising to believe anything. If it's against Bruce, it's not likely I shall. But I'll hear what you've got to say."

They both knew that she believed and that it was the bitterest moment her life had known. But what more was there to say?

Only, as she went out, she heard his assurance: "You know, when you need me, I'm always ready to help."

Yes. She knew that. And even now it was some consolation to hear it said.

CHAPTER XXI.

MURDER!

IT WAS twenty minutes after Mr. Jellipot's usual time for going to lunch. He had just completed a protracted and difficult interview with one of the London and Northern Bank's defaulting customers, and was not entirely satisfied with his own part in the settlement, which had been agreed. He was tired and hungry, and it was with less than his usual patience that he said, when his managing clerk came into the room: "What is it now, Newman? I'm not going to see anyone before three."

But Newman stood his ground. "It's Miss Westerham, sir. She's on the phone. She says it's most urgent."

"Ask her to be good enough to ring up again after lunch."

"I think I'd speak to her, sir. She seemed rather upset."

"It's like that, is it?" He closed the private door which he had half opened. He put his umbrella back into the rack. He picked up the instrument. He heard a voice he knew say: "Could you come at once? Bruce has been killed."

"Do you know by whom?"

"Do you think I'd better say that on the phone?"

"That's a difficult question to answer unless I know more than I do now."

"Well, we're all here: Lady Eleanor, Mrs. Nolan, and I."

"You mean it's been done by one of yourselves?"

"Yes, of course. But I thought you might prefer not to know which one. I know I once heard you say something that—"

"Never mind what you heard. Where are you now?"

"At Lady Eleanor's. It's 6 Belfield Gardens. I expect you know that."

"Have the police been informed?"

"No. Do you think they should?"

"Yes, without delay."

"Well, as long as you'll be here first—"

"I am not sure that it would be wise. Do you wish it to be understood that I shall be representing you, if there should be any occasion to do so?"

"There'll be lots of occasion for that. Yes, of course. And the others as well, if they know what would be best for them."

"I certainly cannot promise that, but I will come now."

He put the instrument down and turned to the waiting clerk: "Newman, someone's murdered Nolan, and she'd rather not say who it is on the phone. Bring me a few biscuits from the tea cupboard, and have a taxi at the door in three minutes."

As he got into the vehicle, he gave the driver five shillings. "It is a matter of urgency," he said. "I rely on you to get me there as quickly as the safety of others and law allows."

A bluff and burly driver looked at him with twinkling eyes. "Right y'are, guv'nor. Leave it to me," he replied, and swung out into the traffic at a pace which confirmed his words. But he had some miles to go through crowded streets, and his passenger had leisure to wonder which of the three women was destined to spend the night in a prison cell.

He told himself that each of them might plead that she had cause enough for the hate from which murder springs. Enough, he thought, to escape the extreme penalty of the law, although much must still depend upon the circumstances of the crime.

There was Lady Eleanor. She had been abruptly made aware of the pit of ignominy into which she had fallen. She would be likely to react most keenly to the dishonour of her position. Who could tell what the result would be? Yet he hoped—he thought—it would not be she.

There was Edith Westerham. She alone had been driven to the degradation of a prison cell. She might claim to have suffered the greatest wrong. Yet again he hoped—he thought—it would not be she. Though who could guess what her thoughts had been surrounded by Holloway's cheerless walls? And she had been released a few hours ago. There was the fact also that it was she who had rung him up. But he saw that there could be no certain significance there.

Finally, there was the original Mrs. Nolan—if first she were. She had, perhaps, the least cause—certainly the least immediate cause—but on the other hand, she was the only one who was attached to the man by a bond which only death or divorce could end. And he could not tell what sudden provocation there might have been. On other grounds, he was conscious that he would prefer it to be she. And had she not said that she had once threatened to put a knife between the ribs of the murdered man? Might she not even now have had murder more or less in her mind? This might emerge when one knew how the murder had been done.

And yet how idle these speculations were! In ten minutes he would know all. So he thought, but on that he was to find himself widely wrong.

The door was opened by a butler whose face was still bloodless from the horror of a scene to which he had been summoned only a few moments before.

"Yes, sir," he said. "It's a terrible thing. The ladies are in the lounge."

"Where is the dead man?"

"They said they'd like you to see them first."

"Are the police here?"

"No, sir. But they've been called. I think that's why they want you to see them at once."

By this time they had gone up the first flight of stairs and were at the lounge door.

Agitation did not affect the formal respect with which the butler announced the solicitor's arrival. "Mr. Jellipot to see you, my lady," he said formally, as he withdrew.

Mr. Jellipot confronted three ladies who looked somewhat calmer and more self-controlled than he would have expected, after what their experiences must have been in the last hour.

Lady Eleanor and Mrs. Nolan sat side by side on a couch, where they were, rather surprisingly, holding hands. Miss Westerham was in a chair by the fire, from which she rose impulsively. "Oh, we're glad you're here first. We've got something important to say—or not to say—to you first. And the police may be here any minute. And Mr. Tarrant and Mr. Tilson are on the way."

"If you would just tell me what has happened as briefly as possible."

"But that's just what we have agreed that it would be silly to do. It would get one of us into a mess, and why should anyone be mean enough to do that?"

"I'm afraid the matter may be too serious to be discussed in that way. You say Nolan is dead?"

"In the dining room. There's no doubt about that."

"How did it occur?"

"He got stabbed with a carving knife. You'll see that, whether I tell you or not."

"Can't you tell me a little more before the police arrive? It will be difficult to deal with the matter in the best way without knowing more than I do now."

"But we thought that, as you are an officer of the Court—you know I understand all about that—you might feel bound to repeat anything that you get from us. And how about being an accessory?"

"I don't think," Mr. Jellipot replied patiently, "that you understand the position accurately. If I should be acting professionally for any of you, whatever I may learn is private, even from the officers of the law, and in any case—"

"But we don't know whether we shall be able to have anyone acting for us, and anyway I suppose that it would have to be Mr. Tarrant for me and Mr. Tilson for Lady Eleanor—we settled this while you were on the way—so that you can say you represent Mrs. Nolan when the police arrive, if you think that's best; but what we've decided to do is to say just nothing at all—I mean nothing about what happened after we got here."

"I think you will find that attitude very difficult for three people to maintain. Even for one, and in less serious circumstances—"

"We don't think it will be easy. We just think it's possible, and we mean to do it. We know it's the right thing. I know enough about being locked up in prison cells for something you haven't done."

"I must suppose that there would be no probability of that occurring. It must surely have been the act of one, unless you mean me to understand that there was a conspiracy to kill him, which I should find it hard to believe."

"But what we want to do is *not* to tell you, and you're trying to lead me on to talk now when I've just said I won't. Eleanor, you can see how it will be. We've got to keep *absolutely* silent, or they'll get everything, bit by bit. But if we do that, there isn't one of us who's got any cause to fear."

As she made this surprising assertion, there was a sharp ring at the bell and, before the front door could be heard to close, it had admitted not only Mr. Truscott, a young man who looked almost frightened at the sudden responsibility which had descended upon him, but Chief Inspector Combridge and two other officers of the law.

The Chief Inspector greeted Mr. Jellipot in the friendly manner natural to their previous contacts. "A bit ahead of us, as usual," he said. "We'd better see the dead man first and then hear the tale. Tonks, you can stay here and see that no one leaves the room till I get back. Rawlings will come with me. Mr. Jellipot, you'd better lead the way, if you will."

"I'm afraid I know nothing more than you do about that."

"You should try the dining room," Edith volunteered. "The second door on the right."

Well, there could be no secret about that; and when the three men entered the room, there could be no doubt that Nolan was dead.

They saw a table laid for three, on which lunch had been served, but remained untouched. They saw an armchair at the head, pushed slightly back and to one side, and a dead man beside it, lying sprawled, face forward, in a pool of his own blood. There was blood also in the slightly hollowed seat of the chair, and on the arm which was nearer to the dead man. The handle of a large carving knife still protruded from his belly, slightly to the right; he was a little on his left side. It must have been driven in with considerable force, and it seemed that when it struck him he must have first fallen across the chair and then slipped to the ground.

"No half-measures here," Combridge said. "Which of them did it?"

"They have decided," Mr. Jellipot replied, "that it is best that they should not say."

"Have they really! We'll soon alter that. I suppose they don't all three want to get hanged."

"It is an improbable supposition, and perhaps an improbable anticipation also."

"You're not backing them up in that?" the Chief Inspector exclaimed, with some surprise and even a faint note of alarm in his voice. "I suppose, if you don't know which of them did it, you could make a good guess?"

"Which it would obviously not be right for me to do."

"Well, have it your own way. Rawlings, I don't think this is going to be one of those cases where you have to look for clues under the mat. Just stay here and touch nothing till Dr. Spekes and the others arrive. I think I can hear them now." He turned to Mr. Jellipot to conclude: "Perhaps we'd better go back and hear what they've got to say."

They went back to the lounge, which was fuller than it had been before. Charles Tilson was there, looking serious but not greatly alarmed. He did not think that his client had committed the crime, and was not sorry that Nolan was dead. If she wished to maintain a silence which was intended to protect the murderess, it would produce an interesting situation, and was an act of chivalry of which he approved, so long as it involved no serious trouble for her. But he did not think it could be successfully done.

As to which of the others had done it—well, it was no business of his. The younger girl seemed to have taken control of the situation. He must just look on, and follow his client's instructions, as long as there was no danger for her.

He observed that Chief Inspector Combridge took the same view as to who controlled the event, for he looked directly at Miss Westerham as he said: "And now, perhaps you'll tell me how this came to happen?"

But it was Mr. Truscott who answered. He had the aspect of a frightened but faithful dog, as he said: "I have advised my client to say nothing at all."

Combridge turned his eyes to the two ladies upon the couch and Mr. Tilson spoke instantly "I am acting for Lady Eleanor, and my advice to her is to say nothing."

Mrs. Nolan looked up. "I'm not going to say anything, except that he deserved what he got and I'm not sorry he's dead."

The Chief Inspector looked round. "I suppose I'm not going to hear that someone's acting for this lady also?"

He thought he would have a negative reply, and had little doubt about who had struck the blow. In a moment the way would be clear ahead.

But Mr. Jellipot surprised himself as he replied: "I think I may say that I am acting for Mrs. Nolan, and my advice to her is that she has already said more than was quite wise, and that she should not add to it in any way."

"Then," the Chief Inspector said with finality, "I shall have to ask you all to come with me to Scotland Yard."

Mr. Jellipot said mildly: "Do you think that that will be really necessary?"

Mr. Tilson was more emphatic. "I should be obliged to advise my client that she is under no necessity to do so. She has a right to decline to answer questions which, for all you know, might incriminate herself, and she can do so just as well here as there."

"They can't all have done it," Combridge replied reasonably. "And unless you're going to tell me that there was a conspiracy to kill him, which I shouldn't believe, they can't all be afraid of incriminating themselves. You know that an innocent person has nothing to fear from us."

"Oh, yes," Miss Westerham interrupted. "I could tell them quite a lot about that."

It was a disconcerting remark, but the officer met it as well as he could by replying: "It was a jury's doing, not ours. You can say it's we who've been active to get you out."

"Yes," she answered, in a rather friendlier tone. "I'm not ungrateful for that. But another jury might go the same way. And besides," she added, with what seemed to him to be a most inappropriate levity, "how do you know that they wouldn't be more nearly right than they were then?"

But lightly though the words might be said, he saw, as did the three lawyers, that she had pointed out the real difficulty that he must confront. No one can be required to incriminate himself. One of the three could be silent, and could be legally advised to be so, with entire propriety. Indeed, all three could be properly so advised if their respective solicitors were not assured of their innocence, as how, in face of such an attitude, could they be?

It might be thought that few innocent women would take the risk of silence to protect one who had committed so foul a crime. But if their sympathies were entirely with her? If—even this was possible—one or both of them were conscious of having had a part in that which provoked the blow?

He said: "Mr. Jellipot, don't you think it might be best to talk this over between ourselves? If you gentlemen will come with me, Tonks can stay here and see that no one leaves till we return."

Mr. Tilson said: "No one will leave. But I must protest against the assumption that my client is not free to go should she wish to do so."

It was evident that he wished to assert that, whoever had struck the blow, Lady Eleanor was above suspicion; but Combridge merely answered: "It is a point of view with which I cannot agree. But your assurance is all I need."

Followed by the three lawyers, he left the room, and returned to that in which the dead man lay, with a doctor now kneeling beside him.

CHAPTER XXII.

A DIFFICULT SITUATION

DR. SPEKES looked up to say: "There's no doubt of the cause of death. It's a case where a child couldn't go wrong. But you'll find it well to have it photographed from every angle, because there's a puzzle about it I can't decide. When he was stabbed, he was facing the table and must have been close to it. There'd have been scarcely space for anyone to have been between him and it, let alone to face him with the knife and use it as she must have done. Unless you get a full confession, you'll have difficulty in reconstructing the crime."

"Quite right, doctor. If it isn't done already, we'll have them from every angle there is. But I'm not worrying about that now. If one of them hadn't killed him, they wouldn't have put up the dumb show we've been watching now. I'll tell you frankly, gentlemen," he continued, turning to the lawyers, "what I'm meaning to do. I can't arrest all three, though I might take them away for questioning, and I may do yet. But I can arrest the one whom I regard as the most probable criminal, and, if one of the others did it, neither of them will be likely for different reasons to keep a shut mouth. If one of them were guilty, would she let an innocent woman hang?"

"She might ask herself first," Mr. Jellipot replied, "whether there would be any danger that you would hang the wrong woman. And while you've not got evidence on which you could even get a committal—"

"It's a bit too early to say that. The fingerprints haven't been tested yet. And we may turn up other evidence, more likely than not. But I think we can all make a good guess at who did it. I mean to run her in and see what happens then."

Mr. Jellipot noticed that the conversation was being left to him, Mr. Tilson acting as though it were a matter in which he could not possibly be concerned, and Mr. Truscott appearing to be too diffident or too discreet for words. But he did not mind that. He made a sound guess that it was his adopted client who was to be selected for the role of murderess, and inwardly he was not disposed to question its probability. He remembered Mrs. Nolan's remark about a carving knife on the previous day. It was partly because of that unsought confidence that he had so readily succumbed to the suggestion that he should act for her. It removed a vexatious doubt, whether it would have been his duty to inform Combridge of what he had heard her say. He asked: "May we be informed who the selected suspect is?"

"I should say the betting on Mrs. Nolan would be about twenty to one."

"Then I must protest that you have no evidence against her whatever, and that of the three she had the least reason for such a crime."

"Well, I say it was she, and when we get the right one locked up, we often find the evidence comes trotting in after."

"If you think you will get a committal simply because you think it was she," Mr. Jellipot replied, "you must be a particularly sanguine man."

The Chief Inspector was not insensible of that aspect of the matter. He knew also that Mr. Jellipot was an opponent to be feared. But what was he to do? He said: "You can't really think that I shall just pick up the corpse, let those three women put their tongues out at us, and walk away?"

"No, I don't suggest that you should. But have you thought that there must be an inquest, unless you ask the coroner to stand back, and that he can require witnesses to give evidence with more authority than the police have?"

The Chief Inspector looked surprised. Was it not against the interests of his client for him to suggest that? But he had done no more than call his attention to something which could not be changed, and which he could not permanently have overlooked. Its immediate result was that the bold and dubious experiment of arresting Mrs. Nolan would be deferred, if not abandoned, which had been the immediate object.

Combridge said: "Well, if we can't get them to talk, it may be best to leave it till then, if we find there's nothing to go on earlier. I must rely on you to keep your clients available."

Mr. Truscott felt that the time for speech had come. He said: "My client is unlikely to go away while she's waiting to hear what compensation she's going to get for the mistake that's been made already."

CHAPTER XXIII.

THE INQUEST

THE office of coroner is recruited from two eminent but distinct professions. Medical and legal gentlemen have separate claims of suitability, which can rarely be united in one individual, and the course of their investigations is inevitably influenced by the angles of their approach.

Dr. Ritchie, being a medical man, though not indifferent to the legal aspects of his enquiries nor ill-equipped to deal with them, was naturally most interested in the physical problems which they presented.

He followed with professional interest the evidence of Dr. Spekes, which to most of those who heard was no more than an inevitable formality (for who could doubt how the man had died?), and when the evidence raised a doubt as to how the blow could have been struck, the point was seized at once for keen analysis and discussion.

In non-technical language, the knife had entered the abdomen slightly to the right of the navel, and slightly below. It had penetrated somewhat upward and to the left, piercing the main artery under the heart with effects which must have been quickly fatal, beyond possibility of relief. That had been easy to see. But if the murdered man had been facing the table, almost close to it, and with the armchair at his right, how and where could the one have stood who had delivered the blow?

Photographs, diagrams, measurements were the subject of close inspections and detailed discussions, which only served to show that there really was a problem difficult to resolve in any plausible way.

The chair, though drawn slightly sideways, had been fairly close to the table, in the normal position for it to occupy before its intended use; and if it could be imagined that the murderess had been wedged closely in a narrow angle between man and chair, with the table behind her, how could she have struck a right-hand blow in the direction the wound had taken?

The coroner, letting his glance fall upon the three witnesses he had called, who were seated together and among whom he had no doubt that the culprit would be discovered, decided that a discreet watch should be kept to ascertain whether any of them used the left hand in abnormal ways. He would give his officer quiet instructions to that effect when this witness left the box.

He observed, with disapproval, that none of the three was taking the enquiry in the mood which he would have chosen to see.

Mrs. Nolan appeared to be merely indifferent—bored would hardly be an unsuitable word to use.

Lady Eleanor looked ill—perhaps too much so to be taking a very lively interest in the scene around her. There might be sufficient explanation of that, without the improbable assumption that it was her hand which had struck that inexplicable blow.

Miss Westerham actually looked amused. He saw her lean forward to Mr. Truscott and say something in a whisper which almost penetrated to where he sat. He had exceptionally good hearing. Had it been: "What fun men are when they get solemn about something they can't guess?" There could be no sense in that. Besides, it verged on contempt of court. Well, she would soon be standing where she would sing to a different tune.

All the same, if he had heard rightly, it meant that one who had almost certainly been there and quite certainly knew what had happened, was finding amusement in the speculations to which she listened. His questions ceased, and as the various legal gentlemen present showed no disposition to probe the medical evidence further, Dr. Spekes left the box and Lady Eleanor Cresswell was summoned to take his place.

She entered the box as one hardly conscious of what she did, and seated herself at the coroner's suggestion in the same indifferent way; but she gave her evidence with a clear simplicity which did not falter in telling of the shame she had undergone.

She told of the ceremony of marriage with the dead man, and said that they had lived happily together until the day of his death. She told how she had heard his true character on that day from her own solicitor's lips, and been constrained to believe it and to recognise that she was not married. And how, after that, she had gone home and heard the tale confirmed by one who was probably his authentic wife.

And then she had had another visitor—another whom he had wronged, and whom his perjured evidence had sent to a jail from which she had only been released a few hours before.

They had talked over what should be done, her own antipathy to public exposure—and sympathy, which might be as bitter to her—opposing Edith Westerham's determination that he should not be left free to betray other women as he had done them.

It was after Miss Westerham's stronger will, and the recognition of her greater wrongs—had she not become an unmarried mother, and with a record of imprisonment, however it might be "pardoned," through the man who posed as Lady Eleanor's loving husband?—had gained reluctant consent to the course of action which she urged, that she had ordered that lunch should be laid for three, Bruce having said that he would not be home before evening, with the intention that her visitors should not leave until she had rid herself of the horror that had entered her life.

When the gong rang, they had gone into the dining room together and, as they did so, Bruce had entered behind them.

But at that point she stopped. She looked at nothing, disregarding questions as though they were unheard.

The coroner said sharply: "Lady Eleanor, you are under no obligation to say anything which might lay you open to a criminal charge, but short of that, it is your duty to assist the court, however reluctant you may be to cause trouble to others. If you should be silent from such a motive, you would become an accessory after the fact, and might yourself become subject to prosecution. Please consider this and the implication that must follow, if you still remain silent."

"I would prefer," she replied, "to say nothing more."

"Then you can stand down."

Mrs. Nolan followed her into the box and gave confirmatory evidence up to the same point, and then, to the coroner's growing exasperation, she became stubbornly silent in the same way.

Edith Westerham came last. Her tale of false evidence, unjust conviction, and prison walls held the attention and gained the sympathy of the crowded court. But when her account of the events leading up to the death of Nolan had reached the point at which her two predecessors in the box had stopped, she too fell silent. The coroner adjured her to be frank, and pointed out that these concerted refusals to give evidence made the most unfavourable impression and might result in severe penalties.

To this she replied with scorn: "Well, you surely couldn't *want* to get anyone into trouble over that lousy hound?"

She may have surprised herself by the vigour of language which exceeded the customary limits of her conversational vocabulary, yet could not fail to be gratified by the murmur of approval which it roused, loud enough to show how many of those who heard were inclined to the same view.

But it ceased abruptly at the coroner's angry rebuke.

"Miss Westerham," he said, "we are here solely to learn the truth. The consequences rest with others. But the law does not allow vengeance to be taken into private hands at whatever provocation, though that may be subsequently taken into account by those who are better equipped than yourself to see where justice and mercy meet. Your conduct, if you are not guilty yourself, is such as to throw suspicion upon two others, of which one must be innocent, and to obstruct the administration of justice, which in itself may bring you within the grasp of the criminal law."

"I have not said I am not guilty," she replied coolly, "I have merely said that I claim my right to say nothing more."

The coroner recognised defeat. He adjourned for lunch.

CHAPTER XXIV.

DR. RITCHIE SUMS UP

AS no sign of left-handedness had been observed in any of the suspects up to the luncheon interval, the coroner gave instructions that they should be under observation if possible during that meal, special attention being given to Mrs. Nolan, who he considered, with much experience and some natural shrewdness to guide him, was almost certainly the one who had used the knife.

Should this observation have an affirmative result, he proposed to call her back to the box, to examine her on the point, and then to sum up in such a way that the jury could not mistake his mind.

As he thought of that summing-up, he was not oblivious of the fact that it would be reported and read even beyond the confines of the English-speaking world. What he would be saying that afternoon would be read by millions on the next day. With such an audience, who would not wish to excel? He made careful notes, even to the neglect of the cutlets upon his plate.

If it were possible, he meant to break down this barrier of aggressive silence: this conspiracy of obvious illegality, which might yet be so difficult for the law to reach.

It would be triumph indeed if, before he left the court, he were able to sign a warrant for the arrest of a guilty woman. That might be beyond his power, for the prerogative of decision was with the jury, but he could at least show his colossal audience that he could handle the matter in the right way.

Returning to court, he was informed that there had been little opportunity for the observation that he had ordered. The three ladies with their solicitors had taken lunch together in a private room which had been engaged for them at the Risdon Bar.

There was certainly nothing of which he could make objection in that, nor could it be said to be in any way contemptuous of the court he ruled, yet it stirred a feeling of resentment in his mind, as emphasising the closeness of the lawless association which it was his business to overcome. And the feeling of being defied, if not contemned, was confirmed by the attitude of those who were now taking their seats. The solicitors had a right to look cheerful, if so they would; but did not the three women behind them appear to have gained in confidence and good spirits? The demeanour of Miss Westerham might be unchanged, for to gild the lily is a proverbially difficult operation, but Mrs. Nolan looked more complacent, as though whatever conversation there had been had done her good, and even Lady Eleanor had a more cheerful mien. Well, it was his business to see that one at least of the three should have cause to look more serious than she did now. That must depend upon how the jury could be influenced by what he was about to say. Turning his eyes upon them and with the thought of his larger audience still in mind, he began his address.

He dealt first with the possibility of suicide, which he dismissed as improbable in itself, by the nature of the inflicted wound, and finally in view of the attitude of those who had knowledge of how he died.

"To be suddenly and unexpectedly confronted," he said, "by three women whom he had deceived and robbed, might be considered a position which would incline some men to an impulse of self-destruction; but, had that occurred, why should those who were present refuse to say what they saw, which might have been entirely beyond their power to prevent? It is a case in which you should find no difficulty in bringing in a verdict of wilful murder. But against whom?

"Against some person unknown? How can you say that, when you know the three—the only three—who were there, one of whom you may consider beyond doubt to have inflicted the fatal blow?

"If you can decide, to the degree of certainty that you require in the affairs of your daily lives, by whatever evidence or deduction, which one of them is the murderess, and which are the two who are conspiring with her to conceal her guilt, you will not hesitate to bring in a verdict accordingly.

"In doing that, you are not required to consider the consequences, which will be in other hands, but only to deliver a true verdict in accordance with the solemn oath you have sworn.

"If you should make an honest mistake, in the absence of that assistance which those who are present here are able and which it is their duty to give, it may well be that justice will still be done, for it is hard to think that a guilty woman would remain silent while an innocent companion were put on trial, and still less so that another innocent one would watch the culmination of such a tragedy without intervention. The conspiracy among the three women—for such it clearly is—to defeat the ends of justice, and make a mockery of the law, is not one which you should condone or support. That, at least, is sure. Beyond that, the responsibility of the verdict is yours, and I can only charge you to obey your consciences and the oath which unites you."

Then, after a short impressive pause, he went on to a detailed consideration of the evidence which the three witnesses had given, dealing with their various wrongs, the circumstances under which they met, and their demeanour under examination. As to Lady Eleanor, did she strike them as the type of woman who would be likely to resort to such violent action? With Edith Westerham he dealt in much the same way, though with no cordiality in his tone. But when he came to Mrs. Nolan, without direct suggestion that she was the guilty party, the scale was pressed gently but firmly down.

Those who would read the charge might approve its tenor, or might observe that a course had been recommended, the legal expediency of which was more evident than its ethical justification. The jury had been invited to make a guess—no doubt the best they could—among the three, in reliance upon the probability that the guilty one (should they have gone wrong) would feel obliged to come forward, or would be denounced by the third.

Mr. Jellipot, listening critically, and warily observant of what any development might mean, not only for those primarily concerned, but for the legal advisers they had enlisted for their limited confidence, reflected that its weakness lay in the fact that it was by its success that it would be most likely to fail. For should they make the correct guess, would not both the others remain silent, and how then would the case be proved?

Chief Inspector Combridge listened to a summing up which he approved. He had a confident anticipation that the jury were going to solve the problem in a way which would relieve his department of the major responsibility for whatever might follow. He had no doubt—there could be none, by irrefutable logic—that the three women had rendered themselves liable to prosecution, one as a murderess and the other two as accessories after the fact. But there was the baffling question of which was which.

He knew that Superintendent Backhouse argued that they had all rendered themselves liable to the murder charge, and he might be right. But he knew also that that was a matter beyond his decision, or even that of an Assistant Commissioner. He knew that the case was engaging the attention not only of the Home Secretary, but of the Law Officers of the Crown, and it was said to be one of which the Attorney General and the Solicitor General did not take quite the same view.

But if he could arrest one of the three for murder on a coroner's warrant, the ground would at once be clear to arrest the other two for their attempt to conceal the crime. And there was additional protection for him and for his department in the fact that on such a warrant an arrest *must* be made. They had no option at all.

He had little doubt that the three would spend the night at their country's cost, and it was a most likely guess that Mrs. Nolan would hold the centre of the picture. He thought there would be mercy for her. It might even be no more than a manslaughter charge, if those who knew what had happened put forward such an account as he thought that Miss Westerham's lively brain would be equal to.

He would be glad to see a judge take a lenient view of her guilt. But his feeling toward Miss Westerham was of a less tolerant kind. He hoped she would get what she deserved, by which he supposed that it would be a long while before she would be a free woman again.

He was rather sorry for Lady Eleanor. She was doubtless dominated by stronger wills than her own. But a good judge would see and doubtless make allowance for that. Now the jury had filed out of the box and Dr. Ritchie had left his seat.

CHAPTER XXV.

IN THE JURY ROOM

A CORONER'S jury differs from that of the criminal courts in two particulars: its number need not be twelve, and a majority verdict is all that is required. It is therefore unusual for its deliberations to be prolonged or for it to fail to reach a decision. But honest men will pause on a difficult case, and opinions may change as arguments will be urged of which some may not have thought before.

It is doubtless the sporting instinct of Englishmen which commits the most momentous decisions, the most intricate legal problems, to the decision of a few randomly selected amateurs, with complete indifference to character, intelligence, or other qualifications. This is the routine of every civil or criminal court. But the coroner's jury with which we are now concerned was fortunately—but for whom?—above the average of its kind.

Its foreman, Mr. Levinson, the managing director of a firm of building contractors and a prominent member of a well-known debating society, was adroit in influencing the views of others and reconciling those who might be most sharply opposed.

Now he looked round the miscellaneous group who had been summoned by the coroner's officer and been unable to dig up any valid reason why they should not be there, and began briskly. "Well, gentlemen, we've got a hard nut to crack, but I daresay our teeth will be good enough. We heard what Dr. Ritchie had got to say, most of which sounded sense to me; but we're not bound by that.

"I suppose we shan't have much difficulty in agreeing that there was murder done, and though the man may have been one of those who are better dead than alive, I suppose that oughtn't to influence us overmuch against putting salt on the right tail—if we can only decide whose that tail is. But I don't want to do all the talking. Let's all say what we think and see how far we are of the same mind."

A voice came from the foot of the table: "Well, it was a nice bit of work, if you ask me. I'd say I'd find something for her to do when she comes out, if I thought I'd be in business that long."

"You have a business in which such assistance would be useful?" Mr. Levinson enquired with an expressionless face, as the other members of the jury turned surprised eyes upon the speaker.

"I'm John Lammy," the man answered, with conscious pride. "Been in business in Long Street for twenty years. I reckon most of you know that."

"Oh, yes. I see." He remembered the sign now. *John Lammy & Co. Family Butchers.* He had an inclination to jest on that ambiguous title, and ask how many families were butchered weekly, which Mr. Lammy's comment upon the lady's homicidal dexterity had certainly invited, but discretion ruled and he went on: "But the first question seems to be which of the ladies used the knife so efficiently. Have you any idea who it might be?"

"I shouldn't say there's much doubt of that. It was the one with the gift of the gab and who'd been in jail. She meant to pay him out the first moment she could, and I don't blame her for that. The law'd given her a raw deal and she thought she could manage her own affairs better than that."

"So you would agree to a verdict of murder against Miss Westerham?"

"No, I wouldn't. Not by a mile. Though I don't suppose she'll get out of it. The police will go about it their own way. But I don't see why we should do their dirty work. I say 'Person unknown'."

"Well," Mr. Levinson said amicably, "you've heard Mr. Lammy's view of the matter. We all know which he means by the one who has the gift of the gab—though we must admit that she, like the rest of them, has got the gift of the not-gab too." He paused three seconds for this mild joke to receive its tribute of smiles, and went on: "But I'll own, if it were left to me to decide, Mrs. Nolan would be my guess. Somehow she looks more the sort, and she may have felt that, as she was the real wife, it was up to her to deal with him as he deserved. That's what I think, but if I called it more than a guess I would go too far."

He was answered by a quiet-mannered, elderly man on his left, a bookseller with a shop three doors from Mr. Lammy's more popular establishment. He said: "I expect we most of us took that view at first, but when I think it over, I'm not so sure.

"We've got to ask ourselves who would be most likely to propose protection of this almost impudent kind and whom the others would be most likely to wish to protect. Don't you think Lady Eleanor fits that description best, and doesn't she look as though she's got most on her mind?"

"I was thinking," an ironmonger on the other side of the table remarked (for it was among the Long Street shopkeepers that the coroner's officer had distributed most of his unwelcome invitations), "much the same thing. But I agree with the chairman that it's no more than a guessing game."

"Well, gentlemen," Mr. Levinson said with a return to his brisker manner, "doesn't it come to this: one of us thinks it was Miss Westerham, but doesn't want to have her arrested when we go back to court, and I'm more inclined to put it on Mrs. Nolan, and Lady Eleanor has got two votes to one. And we can hardly say 'person unknown' when it's about as sure as anything ever was that it's one of the three. Hadn't we better say so and make it clear that we don't know which?

"I am going to propose this: murder or manslaughter by Lady Eleanor Cresswell, Mrs. Lucille Nolan, or Miss Westerham, but there is no evidence to enable us to say which it was.

"I haven't put Lady Eleanor first because she got two votes to the others' one. If I'd meant to go that way about it, I should have taken a proper vote. I've put them in alphabetical order, because that seemed to be the fairest way, and I propose to call Dr. Ritchie's attention to that.

"Now I'm going to put this to the vote and if we agree, some of us may be home before dark."

There was a murmur of assent as he concluded, and without asking for anything more formal than that, he wrote down the verdict and led the jury back into court.

CHAPTER XXVI.

THE ACTIVITIES OF THE CHIEF INSPECTOR

CHIEF INSPECTOR COMBRIDGE considered the verdict of the coroner's jury with agreement but with dislike.

It stated the position in a form which would now penetrate into millions of homes, and the whole nation would see it as a problem which he ought to be able to solve. Difficult? Well, perhaps. But probably plain enough at a close view. And anyway, what is the C.I.D. for? Probably to an expert it would be no problem at all.

His superiors put it to him in much the same way. To take criminal action on the evidence which they now had was a course which the Home office wished to avoid. It was precarious to arrest any one of the three for a murder which could not be proved against her. To arrest the three would be preferable to that, but it would raise novel legal questions with uncertain results.

The Home Secretary took the unusual course of summoning him for a personal talk. He said: "Look here, Combridge, we've considered taking you off this case and putting someone else on, but you've always had the reputation of being a good man, and I'm going to put my money on you. But you've got to bring home the goods. We're not going to let those three women make monkeys of us. We shouldn't if we had to alter the law, but I don't think there'd be any occasion for that. If you can't do anything in the next ten days, we're going to run them in. But we don't want to do that. We rely on you to find us a better way out. We want *some* evidence, however you get it, so that we can make an arrest, and if we get a conviction, we shall have a clear case against the other two."

"Yes, sir, I see that. But if you don't get a conviction? Where should we be then?"

"We should just come out where we walked in. I don't see it as worse than that. But we rely on you to see that we shall not fail. If you get the right one in the cells, she'll break down, more likely than not. And their solicitors must be beginning to wonder how soon they'll be struck off the roll. Can't you talk to *them*, and make them see sense?"

"I have done, more than a bit. But they don't seem to worry. Mr. Tilson told me that the course his client was taking had his entire approval, and he'd put that into writing if I thought it would be any help to have it. Mr. Jellipot almost dared me to arrest Mrs. Nolan, and come unstuck when we'd go into court next morning.

"And it's no good talking to Mr. Truscott. If Miss Westerham told him to forge a cheque, he'd do it, more likely than not. I'm not sure that arresting the wrong one isn't the best chance we've got."

"Well, we can't do that. I mean, not deliberately. But with all the people there are in this now, there must be a weak link, and it's what I trust you to find. I'm going to give you ten days—that's till the House meets—and not an hour more. If you've done nothing by then, we'll arrest the lot. But you'll have lost the best chance that you've ever had."

Combridge retired from this interview with the thought that if it had been decided to put someone else on the job, he could have endured it quite easily. But he knew that, if such a course had been taken and another officer succeeded where he had failed, it would be a matter which it would not be easy to live down. And he certainly did not accept defeat. Again he interviewed the solicitors of the three suspects. He interviewed the suspects themselves. He knew that the longer people talk, the greater is the probability that the careless or foolish word will be said, which will lead to the disclosure of further things.

He listened to Superintendent Backhouse, who did not cease to urge his advice: "Fetch one of the bitches in, and in forty-eight hours you'll have learnt all that there is to know."

But that was a course which, without supporting evidence, he had been forbidden to take, and Mr. Jellipot's warning was in his ears.

Yet he considered the three candidates for the dock, one by one, in the role of culprit or of decoy.

Taking them in the order of their connection with the dead man, Lucille was first on the list. Regarding her, he had discovered, and then probed, one surprising fact. Her employers, a small firm of export merchants, had taken her back in spite of the way in which she had treated them. More than that, they had installed her in a better position than she had held previously. When he called on her there, he found that she had been given a private office. The name painted on the door was still wet.

She had not declined discussion but had been abrupt and blunt. Whether or not she had used the knife, she did not express less than satisfaction with the use to which it had been put.

"I once threatened him myself," she said, "with one nearly as good. You won't get more out of me than that, if you sit here for a week. But why worry about the swine? You're enough to make a saint swear. Why not worry a bit more about the children the lorries kill?"

As she talked thus, she had seemed the most likely suspect of the three, as perhaps she was; but, had she been guilty, would she have spoken so boldly? He doubted that.

And as to her improved position in the firm, there was an explanation, about which no reticence was shown by any of those concerned. She had invested £1,000, which the firm had been glad to have. It was the money which Nolan had given her and which Lady Eleanor had refused to take back, saying with literal truth that it had not been hers.

Had this been a bribe to secure silence? It was open to that construction. But Lady Eleanor was a wealthy woman. It could mean little to her. And it was true that she had given it to Nolan absolutely. Her distaste—her refusal—to consider taking it back was natural enough. He felt he could not make much of that against either of them.

As to Lucille, he felt he had drawn a blank, and Edith Westerham was next on the list.

Finding on enquiry that she was not now living at Ashfield Terrace, but had returned to Miss Manly after Holloway had opened its gates for her release, he saw that he had the choice of calling upon her either there or at Mr. Jellipot's office. But it was afternoon when he left Mrs. Nolan. When he enquired at Ashfield Terrace (where he would have preferred to await her) it was too late to return to the city, and with a ten-day limit upon his mind, he resolved to go at once to Miss Manly's Jordans home. But this could not be quickly done. It involved a bus to Marylebone, a train journey to Beaconsfield, another bus journey, and, as he subsequently found, a walk of about a mile.

When he got there, Miss Westerham, who had travelled by the previous train, was just rising from her evening meal, as Miss Manly, who faced the window, said: "There's your friend Combridge coming up the drive."

"I wonder whether he's come to arrest me. They're bound to do something soon. I suppose I've got to see him, if so. But I'd much rather not. I'm sick of saying I won't say."

Miss Manly, glancing at her, could see that she was strained and tired, and judged her to be physically unfit for a further sparring-match with the law. She said, as the bell rang in the hall: "Well, why should you? Go upstairs and I'll deal with him."

Somewhat reluctantly, for it was not her habit to decline the challenge of battle, but aware that there was no time for hesitation, Edith said: "Oh, it's kind of you, if you will," and had gained the stairs and rounded their first turn, before the door opened to admit her persecutor.

"Show the gentleman in here, Mary," Miss Manly said, as she crossed the hall and entered a small room, half-office, half-library, which was private to her own use.

"Miss Westerham?" she was saying next moment. "No, I'm afraid you can't. She was tired when she came in and she's gone up now. Is there any message I can give her?"

"No. I wanted to see her about the trouble she's making. We shall he bound to make some arrest if it goes on many days longer, and we'd rather get her to talk sensibly without that if we could. Perhaps," he added, adjusting his mind to the position that confronted him, "you could persuade her to see it in the right light?"

He was seated now in a leather-backed chair which was comfortable though scarcely luxurious, and Miss Manly had taken one with a straighter back which fronted her desk.

She looked at him with the shrewd, very blue eyes which were the attraction of an otherwise plain face, as she answered: "Of course, I should be glad to do that. But are you sure what the right light is?"

"I should have thought there could be no doubt about that. Unless she did it herself—which you may know better than I—it is her evident duty to tell us what happened."

"As to that, I can assure you that I know no more than yourself, and it is therefore a very difficult matter on which to offer her any advice."

"I shouldn't have thought that you would be one to approve of that kind of violence."

"You would be quite right. I don't approve of violence at all. But are you sure that, if she were to tell you that she killed Nolan, the law would do no violence to her?"

"Well, I don't make the laws and it's not really my business to answer that. But I should say that, if she could give a good account of how it happened, so that it wouldn't look as though she came out of jail, so to speak, with a knife in her hand, she might get off fairly lightly."

"Aren't we speaking rather as though we had concluded that she did it herself, which I certainly do not accept as probable? But I'll tell you this: I do not approve of the course which was taken, and any influence I might have would be on the side of the truth being plainly told. But Miss Westerham has been treated so badly, both by Nolan and by what I considered to be an incompetent court, that if I hadn't stood by her at one time, she might not have had a friend in the world. And whatever she says or doesn't, this house will always be a home for her."

"Well, I see how you feel; but what I said was meant for her own good."

"And you can depend upon my telling her that," Miss Manly replied in her pleasantest manner, but rising with the words, so that her visitor could understand that the interview was over and get what satisfaction he could from the conclusion that Miss Manly was more or less on his side.

It was too late to do more that night, but he went to Belfield Gardens next morning, reminding himself cheerfully of the proverb that the third try pays for all, and with some anticipation that Lady Eleanor might not be too resolute to be overcome.

But his repulse here was more absolute than that which he had encountered the night before. The butler he already knew informed him, with bare civility, that Lady Eleanor was not at home. A suggestion that he would await her return was met by a frigid reply that it might not be worth his while to do so. A request to know what time would be likely to suit her convenience was repulsed in an equally negative way.

With some natural annoyance and an equally natural ignorance of the fact that Mr. Tilson was at that moment in conversation with her in the first-floor lounge, he decided to see her solicitor, in the expectation that he might change the attitude of that aloof gentleman by using plainer words than he had yet done.

So he went into the city and, on arriving at Cole and Tilson's offices, he was spared enquiry by hearing a young clerk inform a coal-black gentleman, very lavishly dressed, that Mr. Tilson would not be back before lunch, and was uncertain for the rest of the day.

Could he be expected to connect the top-hatted Negro with the business which brought him there? It is unreasonable to suggest. Yet it was a fault of imagination which he would afterwards much regret.

CHAPTER XXVII.

A Bargain with the Police

"IT WAS kind of you to come," Eleanor said gratefully. "But there is nothing that I can tell you. We have promised each other most explicitly that we will say nothing which might mean trouble for the others."

"On the contrary, if you all remain silent, I think it must mean trouble for all, two of whom should not have had any, and the third may find her position worse than it need have been."

"Why should there be trouble for all?"

"Because the police will not let it rest as it is. I think that is practically certain. They will either arrest one or three, and I should say it's an even chance which."

"If I thought that, I should—" She pulled herself up sharply, and if Charles Tilson saw significance in that unfinished remark, he gave no sign of his thought.

He said: "Well, you *can* think it. And I want you to tell this to the other two: if they had nothing to do with the murder, they're quite right not to tell their solicitors that, which would place them in a position of embarrassment, but the one who did it ought to be frank with hers. It will be confidential, and enable him to advise her in the right way. But I didn't come to talk about that. I came to say that I've been a fool, and I only hope you'll forgive me now."

"You know there's nothing to forgive. You've always been my best friend."

"I've been more than that. I've loved you since we first met. And I think there was a time—I don't know how it is now—when you felt the same. And because of the wretched money, I was too cowardly to say anything. And so you married that bounder—"

"I didn't *marry* him. You know it was worse than that."

"I don't see much difference. Especially now he's dead. The question is, will you marry me?"

"How *could* I, after what's happened? And you not knowing how soon I might be hanged!"

"Eleanor! If that's all the objection you've got, it's the best thing that you've ever said. If you love me, do you think anything else matters?"

"Oh, Charles! Charles! How can you?" she cried, and burst into a passion of bitter tears, which were slow to cease, even when his arms were round her and he was kissing the head that she turned away.

It was at this moment that there was a discreet knock at the door; he crossed the room quickly before anyone could enter and gave the instruction which turned the Chief Inspector away.

But that gentleman had a pleasant surprise when he returned disconsolately to Scotland Yard, feeling that the second of the ten days was passing with nothing done, for there was a message from Cole and Tilson upon his desk asking him to call upon them at 3:30 that afternoon, which he was punctual to do.

He was shown into Mr. Tilson's office at once and greeted in a very friendly manner, but one which left the opening gambit to him.

"I understand," the solicitor said, "that you have been asking to see me."

"Yes. I hoped that you might be able to influence your client, so that she would abandon her present attitude, and might perhaps persuade the others in the same way. It will lead to very serious trouble for all of them if they continue in their present silence."

"And if they don't? Can I say that there will be no trouble then?"

"I cannot possibly promise that in view of what one of them must have done."

"But for the other two?"

"I think there might still be time for frank statements to be accepted. Of course, they would have to repeat them in the witness box without any more dodging."

"You mean if one of them should be put on trial for Nolan's death?"

"Yes, of course."

"And otherwise?"

"I don't see how there could be any otherwise."

"It may not be an unreasonable view. But if I make a bargain, I like it to be free from ambiguities."

"You mean you're offering a deal?"

"Not exactly. I'm asking whether an offer is being made. If I try to get you something you want, I must know what the conditions are: what I can offer, to persuade the ladies or their legal advisers in the right way. There'd be a time limit, of course."

Chief Inspector Combridge considered this with a better hope than he had yet had. It seemed to him that the solicitor was offering the disclosure of the murderess, on condition that her companions should not be brought to account for the delay which had occurred, and the price did not seem high to him.

But had he the right to make such a bargain? Remembering the time limit under which he himself was acting, he thought he had. The ten days were now eight. If, when the House should meet, an arrest had been made, based on a confession by the guilty woman and supported by the evidence of her companions, he thought that even without such a stipulation there would be no inclination on the part of his superior officers to prosecute those on whom their case would so largely depend. And if pressure were to be put upon them to induce them to talk, was it not reasonable that those who were to exercise it should be able to tell them what the consequences would be? He said: "If it isn't more than a week—"

"I am willing to agree to that. I will send you a letter to that effect."

"There's no need for that. You know you can take my word."

"So I do. And so I should if I were the principal. But I must pledge myself to others, which is a different matter. And I shall not go beyond the exact terms we have now agreed. If you dislike my letter, you can repudiate anything you have said now. I shall do nothing whatever till I get your reply, which, by the way, should be addressed to the firm, not to myself."

"That sounds right enough. But am I to do nothing in the meanwhile? And if I don't, can I expect to get something worth having from you?"

"I can promise nothing. But you can suppose that I am not making such a proposition without reason to anticipate that I can carry it through, and, if I don't, you can arrest all three on the next day so far as I am concerned. Of course, I don't—"

He stopped suddenly, as though conscious of indiscretion in what he had been commencing to say. The Chief Inspector showed a quick wit, which was not always his strongest suit, in seeing the weakness of the bargain which he had been so near to exposing.

He said: "Of course, there'd have to be a promise that they wouldn't go off in the meantime."

"Do you think I could pledge that?"

"I don't see how we can agree on anything if you can't."

"Perhaps a formula which would meet your difficulty would not be impossible. Shall we say that if any one of the three shall go five miles outside the metropolitan area before a full confession, with supporting statements, is in your hands, you will be free to act as you will?"

"That sounds fair enough," he replied, though in the hesitant tone of one who was still not entirely easy in mind.

"Very well. I will write to you this afternoon."

The Chief Inspector walked away in a thoughtful mood but not discontent He decided wisely to make a full immediate report of what he had done. Indeed, the letter which would soon be on its way gave him little option on that. Also, as he was content to see, the bargain would not be made without official approval. The credit of success would still be his, while the responsibility for any complication—but what could there be?—would not lie at his door alone.

He reported what he had done, which was well received. He mentioned that faint shadow of doubt which had come to him as the conversation had neared its end. He said: "You don't think Tilson could have any trick up his sleeve to get the woman away before we could run her in?"

The Assistant Commissioner was not worried by that possibility. He said: "We must keep too good a watch on them for that. And where could she go? She pleads guilty if she bolts, whether she's made a confession or not, and extradition treaties should do the rest. But all the same we'll leave nothing to chance. We'll stipulate that their passports shall be surrendered. Beyond that, we must wait to see what his letter says."

The letter came next morning, and was as explicit as could be desired. It read:

Re Nolan deceased.

Confirming our conversation with Chief Inspector Combridge this afternoon concerning the manner of the death of the above, it is agreed that we shall make our best endeavours for one week from this date (not including the date hereof) to procure for you a signed statement admitting responsibility therefore, and the confirmatory statements of two witnesses, on the explicit conditions that (1) the three ladies in question, Mrs. Bruce Nolan, Miss Edith Westerham, and Lady Eleanor Cresswell, shall not be subject to any interference from the police until the expiration of the above-mentioned period, or until the above-mentioned documents shall be in your hands, whichever period may be the shorter; and (2) apart from direct complicity in the death of Nolan, none of them shall be subject to any penalty or process of law in respect of any reticence they may have shown prior to the statements which it is now proposed to secure, providing that such reticence be not continued beyond the time limit of this letter.

It is understood that, should any of the ladies above-mentioned go, at any time during the coming week, more than five miles beyond the limits of the metropolitan area, without your knowledge and consent, all undertakings in this letter, and in your reply thereto, will be voided thereby.

Yours faithfully,

Cole and Tilson
C. T. Cole

After some hours of careful consideration, during which the terms set out had secured the approval of the law officers of the Crown, a reply was sent confirming the bargain, subject to the surrender of passports, about which no difficulty was to supervene; and the Chief Inspector very willingly turned his attention to other matters, while the very competent officers who had been detailed to watch the three women made their regular reports. They showed no sign whatever of a disposition to interrupt the routine of their daily lives, apart from some inclination to risk the hazards of matrimony, which may be indulged within the prescribed metropolitan limit and often is.

CHAPTER XXVIII.

MAINLY CONCERNING MABUDALAND

AFTER Combridge had left the solicitor's offices, Charles Tilson strolled into his partner's room.

"Busy?" he asked, as he sat down, leaning back comfortably in a well-padded chair and stretching out his long legs before him, as one who had settled down for unhurried talk. "Well, I'm glad you're not. Do you think Lady Eleanor could lend me £50,000?"

"Yes, if you asked. And she would forget it in the next hour. But it would take a few days to raise."

"That wouldn't matter at all."

"May I ask why you require so considerable an amount?"

"Hastings is coming on well. I thought you might agree to my disposing of my partnership to him. He has made me a very fair offer."

"I should have thought that such a course would put a substantial sum into your pocket, rather than entail the borrowing of another."

"You mean the £50,000? Oh, I shall need that as well. I really only wanted to know whether it could be raised quickly. You see I'm going to marry her during the next day or two, and it may be useful."

"Charles," Mr. Cole said kindly, "I may regard as mere details that you should propose the dissolution of our partnership and undertake a somewhat abrupt marriage, but would you mind telling me what has been distracting your mind for the past week?"

"That was what I was proposing to do. Have you ever heard of Mabudaland?"

"Yes. Everyone has during the last few months. But I can make an easy guess that I know much less than you."

"Well, you know that the British Government, using the pruning knife which is the only tool they keep sharpened at the Colonial

Office now, has granted the natives there their independence, and Chief Ajubi has been appointed its first President."

"Yes. And apart from the fact that it's in the highlands of central Africa, that's about all I do know."

"Well, the new President has been looking out for a legal adviser, who's to be Attorney General or something of that sort when he gets organised, and I've got the job."

"What kind of legal advice will he want from you?"

"Oh, to draft bills mostly, as far as I can make out. He's going to have a parliament and enough laws that they don't understand to teach the Mabudas what democracy really means."

"Charles, I wonder whether you've considered that there won't be any extradition treaty with this country yet, more likely than not?"

The eyes of the two men met with an understanding that went beyond spoken words.

"No," he said. "I know there isn't. I start from scratch. But I expect I shall be asked to advise on one which will be drafted here."

"So that, if there should be a retrospective clause, you could strike it out?"

"Yes. I should be able to see objection to that."

"I've no doubt you would. It's a healthy climate?"

"Excellent in the hills. Anyway, so I'm told. Baboons thrive."

"Do you mind telling me how she did it? I needn't say it won't go outside this room."

"How or why?"

"Both, by choice."

"Well, I think the trouble was that she really loved him. She was hurt twice over. It wasn't only her pride. And what those two women told her changed that love to loathing. You know, Lucille had reacted in much the same way. She told him she'd use a knife if he put his hands on her again.

"So, in that mood, she went into the dining room with the other two; she had reached the head of the table and was just pulling out her chair to sit down, when he came in.

"When he saw the three together, he must have guessed that exposure had come, but I think he relied on having a hold on her that she couldn't break, and he thought he could do anything with women. You couldn't blame him for that. So he tried, even then, to bluff it out. He came up behind her, with a joking word, and pulled her head round for a kiss. In the fury it roused she snatched at the carving knife that was near her hand and thrust it backward, not caring where it went so long as it ended his handling her. Thrust backward in her right hand, you can see how it would go in."

"Yes. I see that. If you annoy her seriously, you'll know what to expect. But I wouldn't say she didn't do the right thing. Of course, that's strictly between ourselves. But won't you leave the two others in a rather bad hole?"

"No, I think our friend Combridge is helping me out of that."

"You'll have to be careful with him. He's not brilliant, but he's very slow to let go."

"Well, I'll tell you what the deal is, and you can O.K. the letter before it goes."

Mr. Cole listened with care and approved with reservations.

He asked: "If it should leak out that you're leaving the country? Wouldn't you be in the soup then?"

"I don't think it will. I've stipulated for absolute privacy till I've settled up business matters here, and they're too keen on getting me not to keep their word. Actually, there are only two Mabudas in London and neither speaks English well enough to get really chatty with anyone. They've opened the Mabudaland Embassy at their lodgings in Pembury Road, S.W."

"Well, you should know what you're doing. But as for getting £50,000, let alone the rest of her money, out of the country, have you thought that that may be a lot harder than bolting yourselves?"

"It won't be any trouble at all. The Board of Trade has given a licence to the new state to purchase up to £200,000 worth of agricultural machinery and other goods in this country, providing that sterling to pay for it is in London before shipment. It's probably more for the sake of the cash I can lend them than admiration for my capacity to draft laws, that they've made the deal."

"You don't propose to make any secret about the marriage?"

"No, why should we? When Combridge hears of it, as I bet he will within half an hour, he'll think he's got the explanation of why I'm trying to clear the thing up. I expect he'll think it shows that I know Eleanor didn't use the knife. He'll be half right and half wrong, and we know that nothing ties a man up worse than that."

"Well, I must wish you luck, though I can't say that we shall not miss you here."

"If you could wish me forty-eight hours to the day, it would be what I need most."

"Then you'd better stop talking now."

CHAPTER XXIX.

MARRIAGES

MR. JELLIPOT finished his dictation, and his stenographer closed her notebook and rose to go. But he said: "Wait a moment, Miss Westerham. I've heard something from Mr. Tilson that you may be interested to know. He's marrying Lady Eleanor at eleven today."

Edith was not quick to reply. It seemed that she could not instantly adjust her mind to all the implications and consequences of what she heard, but an association of ideas caused her to glance down at the hand which held the closed book, and Mr. Jellipot, an erratically observant man, saw that there was a wedding ring where it is usual for that symbol of marriage to be.

Mildly surprised, and dismissing from his mind a momentary idea that it might be lingering evidence of her irregular connection with a dead man, he said: "May I conclude that he is not the only one who has just experimented in that way?"

"Yes. I'm Mrs. Truscott now. That was why I asked for time off yesterday morning. I should have told you, but you were busy with more important matters."

"You should have done so. The question of relative importances might have appeared to me as it doubtless did to you. I must congratulate Mr. Truscott. I am sure that you have made him a happy man."

"Well, he seems cheerful enough. I wouldn't say he's got Bruce's technique, but I didn't want a second helping of that." A smile curved her lips and amusement was in her eyes, at recollections which she certainly did not intend her employer to share.

"I must conclude that it was rather quickly arranged?"

"Yes, I told him what he was in for on Sunday. I didn't know that Eleanor would try the same thing, but it seemed a good business to me. It put him in the clear whatever I might feel obliged to tell him to do; and when you've got a lawyer who'll do anything you ask, however silly for him—well, it seemed the fairest way out."

"I am sure you had other motives than that."

"Yes, lots. But that was in the pack. And Eleanor must have seen it the same way. If Mrs. Nolan had the sense—"

She checked herself, as nearly confused as it was in her nature to be, as she realised the implication of what she said.

But Mr. Jellipot understood what was left unsaid and replied without taking offence. "If you are suggesting that it might be to Mrs. Nolan's advantage that I should marry her, I must assure you that the question has not arisen in any form. It would involve an intimacy which would, I am sure, be as uncongenial to herself as to me. But I think you may be disposed to exaggerate the legal advantages which you have been so expeditious to secure. Which brings back to my mind that Mr. Tilson has asked me to release you for an hour or two this afternoon, so that you may discuss a proposition which he will put to you at his office, when, if I understood him correctly, the other ladies will also be present.

"I must assume that he will propose that you should join in a statement which will put an end to a situation which even a plurality of marriages will not indefinitely sustain. It is a reasonable forecast that Mrs. Nolan will be invited to admit what she has done. I have given consent to her attendance without my presence, both because I have an absolute confidence in Mr. Tilson's judgment, and because I do not wish to be a party to the conspiracy of silence which in the privacy of this office I may suppose to have originated with yourself."

Mrs. Truscott said: "Well, you seem to have thought it all out," but while there was no lack of respect in her voice, there was a hint of mockery in her eyes which caused him to reply mildly: "And, as usual, I shall find that I have been wrong. But I believe I am not mistaken in supposing this to be an occasion on which a gift may be accepted without inferences or obligations attaching thereto."

As he said this, he filled in a cheque for £25 to the order of the name she had just acquired.

"It is also an occasion which is often celebrated by taking a vacation which, even at such short notice, I should not refuse. But perhaps, under the somewhat unusual circumstances—?"

"Oh, yes," she replied. "Till it's all cleared up, we shall just stay put and go on as we are."

"Then let us hope that that will not be a distant day."

CHAPTER XXX.

CONFESSION

CHARLES TILSON and his four-hour wife sat at one side of the table and Edith Truscott faced them. They had discussed the weather, the jewel robbery at the Grand Astor Hotel, the dollar crisis, and the unsuitability of Mr. Ramsay MacDonald to control the destinies of the British people, but still Mrs. Nolan did not appear.

They had telephoned her office and ascertained that she had left by taxi more than an hour earlier. The two ladies who were present were confident that she would not decline to cooperate in the plan which was now proposed. They could make no suggestion as to what could delay her now.

Charles Tilson had already put many urgent matters aside for this, which had seemed to him to be the most important of all. He had typed three long documents with his own hand, feeling that their contents could not be disclosed to the most reliable secretary, and not having thought early enough of the possibility of enlisting Mrs. Truscott's more capable fingers. Now he said: "Well, we can't wait for ever. I'll read over what I've got down, and you two can sign or amend anything that I've got wrong."

He read a sufficiently circumstantial admission of what had happened for his wife's approval and signature, to which she did not demur. He then read a confirmatory statement, which he had prepared in duplicate for the signatures of her companions. Edith said: "Yes, that's right enough. It almost sounds as though you were there," and pulled out her pen.

As she signed, the door opened at last, but it was not Mrs. Nolan, but Mr. Cole who entered the room.

He said: "There's been a queer development, but there's no reason why you shouldn't all hear what it is. I've got Combridge on the phone, and he seems happy enough, except that he's very anxious that we should agree that he's not breaking faith with us. He was told that you were engaged but, of course, not who you've got here.

"The fact is that Mrs. Nolan has gone to Scotland Yard and coughed everything up."

Eleanor went very pale and looked at her husband as though to ask what even he could do now. She said: "Well, if she's done that!"

Edith said bitterly: "I don't believe it. It's what Lucille never would. You'll find there's dirty work somewhere. It just shows what the police are."

Mr. Cole said: "She may have misunderstood the purpose for which she was asked to come here. But I can't see why you should mind, if Combridge keeps his bargain with you, as he says he will."

Charles asked: "You say he's on the phone now?"

"Yes, he's waiting to speak to you."

"Then I'll hear what he's got to say."

After that they listened to the one-sided conversation which can be so maddening to those whom it half informs, and can so largely mislead. "That you, Combridge? Yes, Tilson. Do I understand that you've got Mrs. Nolan at the Yard, and she's made some statement to you? Well, I don't agree. I think you should have refused to take it, in view of the bargain we had made. You couldn't? Of course you could. She says *what*? Why not read it to me, and I shall be better able to judge." After that, there was a long silence, broken occasionally by: "You might read that again," or "Yes, I've got that." And then, the reading of the statement being concluded, the conversation resumed. "What you mean is that our bargain stands? There's no restriction at all? No, you couldn't say less than that. Very well, we'll go on to the end of the week, keep our own bargain or what's left of it, and just call it a day."

He hung up and lifted his eyes to his companions.

"Mrs. Nolan," he said, "has confessed. She has given a circumstantial account of how Nolan was killed by her. The police are holding her, as we must expect them to do. Combridge says that there was no move of any kind on their side to induce or influence her, in view of their agreement with us, but what she offered they could not refuse to take. He says that you are both at full liberty to do as you will, even the condition of the five-mile limit being withdrawn, and your passports will be returned."

Edith began to speak and checked herself at the first word.

Eleanor looked at her husband, as though for some comfort she could not reasonably expect. She said: "Charles, what shall we do? We can't possibly allow that."

He answered her: "Darling, don't worry more than you can't help. We'll find a way through. But I can't suggest anything till I know what the facts really are. Mrs Truscott, you're the only one who hasn't yet confessed anything, will you please tell us how you killed Nolan and why?"

Edith was slow to answer. She looked grave and worried. Then her face broke into a sudden smile. "You'd better ring up the inspector to say that I've just confessed, and if he likes he can come here and I'll tell him how it was done."

Charles said shortly: "There's no need for that. You can tell him on the telephone, if you really mean what you say."

"You don't believe me?" she retorted, with lifted brows. "Then don't you see that I've got to have time to think? I can't make it up as I go along."

"It's too late for humbug, Mrs. Truscott. Eleanor, if you love me, tell me what really happened, and then we can think out what's best to be done."

"There's no doubt about that, Charles. It happened just as you've got it down."

"Then why should this infernal fool go to the station and queer the pitch as she has?"

"I think it was because she thought that they were going to be told it was I, and didn't understand that we might get away, and she'd rather be the one to be blamed."

"Then tell me who proposed this cockeyed plan that's got us all where we are now?"

"It was Mrs. Nolan, of course. She said, almost as she saw him fall over the chair: 'Good for you!' or something like that. 'I'd have done it, if he'd tried the same thing with me. You needn't be afraid we'll give you away.' And then we talked over how it would be possible for it not to come out; and Edith said if we'd all got the guts not to talk, she didn't see how anyone could tell what had happened. She said: 'They won't hang us all three,' and it was arranged that way. They made me swear to say nothing unless one of them should be actually convicted, because, they said, when it had once been started, it would only make trouble for them'."

Her eyes turned to Edith for confirmation, which was quickly given. "Yes, that's how it was; and I still think if we'd all played the game, we should have come through. Fancy them putting us in the dock for murder, and asking any jury to convict all three, when they'd heard the kind of swine that he was!

"And I can tell you that prison isn't so bad—not if you can stand being cooped up. You're like a well-kept beast. Better fed than many people outside. If you co-operate, they treat you quite decently."

"But, Mrs. Truscott," Charles said, with difficult patience, "the question isn't what would have happened; it's what will happen now."

"Then I say that mayn't be much to worry about, even yet. The police say they'll leave us alone till the week ends. What I've signed there's the truth. You've got their letter, that lets me out. It's your job to get Eleanor safely away and send in the statements. You can't do better than that."

"And Mrs. Nolan?"

"They can't do much to her after they've got our accounts. They can call me as a witness, as I shall remain here, but what good shall I be to them? They'll just throw their hand in and let her go. Besides, she's played this ball off her own bat, and we shall have done all we can."

Charles looked at his wife, and the eyes that met his were doubtful and troubled, but Mr. Cole said: "If we've got the real truth at last, I don't see what better, or indeed what else, you can do. You know, Charles, your first duty is to get Eleanor safely away, and any hour you might find that to be a harder job than it sounds now."

Edith said: "If that's how it's to be, and there is no more to do now, I'll get back. As it is, I expect Mr. Jellipot will have to stay till about seven, if he's to sign his letters tonight."

Saying which, she rose, declining even to wait for one of the cups of tea which were approaching the door, said goodbye and good luck, and was quickly in the descending lift.

CHAPTER XXXI.

HESITATIONS

LEFT alone, the three conspirators looked at one another during a short silence.

Then Charles said doubtfully: "I don't like it, but I suppose we're really safe enough till the week ends, if Mrs. Nolan doesn't alter her tale."

"Oh, she won't do that," Eleanor said confidently, but she saw she spoke to those who were not equally sure.

"It's like this," Mr. Cole said, "the police will go on questioning her, and if she's not made up an *absolutely* watertight lie, they'll notice some little discrepancy and get working on it. If it gives them the least idea that they're being led up the garden path—well, there's no telling where it will end. But I agree with Charles that we can't help that, and the only question is how soon you can get away."

Then he added doubtfully: "I suppose there's no refuge possible with the Mabuda Embassy? You said they'd got one, silly as it all sounds."

"Yes," his partner answered, with equal doubt in his voice. "They think they have, though I'm not sure even of that. I've put in an application to the Foreign Office that Mr. Yubo be recognised as Envoy Plenipotentiary and so on for the new state, and they didn't say no. The fact is, they didn't know *what* to say. Giving Mabudaland its independence is just a step lower in breaking up the British Empire than the Colonial Office has gone before.

"They indicated at last that he might probably be recognised with a more modest title than I suggested, which was what I expected to hear, but it's silly not to ask for more than you're sure to get.

"The point is that I haven't yet got a written reply. Mr. Yubo and his colleague have got two rooms, as I told you, in Pembury

Road. By international usage they should be extraterritorial and Eleanor should be as safe there as though St. Peter had let her in.

"But there's the doubt. And another point that might be much worse. Suppose I take Eleanor there, and the police should stop at the door, and respect Mr. Yubo's rights? Would we like to stay in those two rooms for the rest of our lives? Or how would we get away?"

"Yes. It's certainly a difficult point," Mr. Cole agreed, "though I suppose that the rooms might become four, or even the whole house and the one beyond. But what I was thinking was that if the police did ignore any protest and just butt their way in and take her away, it would be a matter for a Privy Council appeal, with the Government liable to be ridiculed through the whole world. I don't think they would risk that."

"I know I shouldn't anyway," Eleanor said, with more decision and more buoyancy than she had yet shown. "But you seem to be forgetting that we've got a box for *The Taming of the Shrew* tonight, and that we've got to get home first.

"I can't really see that there's overmuch to worry about, and I say let's go as we planned, especially as I've asked the Truscotts to join us there."

"Yes, Charles," Mr. Cole added, "I think that's the right course to take. And it's a play which may give you some hints that you shouldn't miss."

"Charles knows how to get his way quite well enough without that," she answered, with the recovered lightness of tone that it was pleasure to hear. "He won't see anything tonight that he doesn't know. But I've asked the Truscotts to join us, and if Edith can get away in time, she may find that it teaches her captive to wag his tail in a different way from what he does now."

So they went out in good spirits enough, happily unconscious of what was being said in a room at Scotland Yard, less than two miles away.

CHAPTER XXXII.

MRS. NOLAN MUST THINK AGAIN

SUPERINTENDENT BACKHOUSE considered the statement that Mrs. Nolan had signed.

He read it with care and a particularly expressionless face. He decided that it was probably of substantial accuracy, in that it recorded what Mrs. Nolan had said. He knew that Combridge could be relied on for that. That Mrs. Nolan's natural words had been systematically changed, "We went into the dining room" being altered to "We proceeded" in that direction, was recognised as being no more than translation into the language which they considered suitable for the written word.

But her account remained vivid and clear. She said that intense feeling against the man who had betrayed them had been generated by the discussion they had had upon their different wrongs. She had not expected him to appear when he did. She had been told that he would not return till evening.

She had told him before then that he should never lay hands on her again; she had even threatened him with a knife. But when he came in, he had the effrontery to attempt to win her over, to assume (did he rely on that £1,000?) that she would be loyal to him. He may have thought that it was from her that his greatest danger would come, which was largely true. Anyway, so it had been.

She was not sorry that he was dead. She would never say that. But she could not agree that her fellow victims should make further sacrifices for her. So she told the truth now, though she had been over-persuaded to silence before.

As the Superintendent read this circumstantial narrative the first time, he had no doubt that it was true, but after he had considered it further there was so long a silence that Combridge said at last, in some impatience: "Well, what do you make of it? I should say that we're home, at a good guess."

"I think," Superintendent Backhouse answered deliberately, "that it shows that she didn't listen very intelligently to the medical evidence."

"What's the point of that?"

"Only that she didn't do it."

Comprehension was not slow to come to the Chief Inspector's mind. In an instant he remembered her description of how the blow had been struck—he remembered and understood. No one likes to feel that he has exposed himself to the accusation of being densely stupid, and this is specially true of the C.I.D. He said frankly: "Of course you're right. I was rather thick in the head not to see that before."

"Oh, I wouldn't say that. Why should she confess, if she didn't do it? It's the sort of thing that you don't think to question, unless you run across a snag that you can't shift."

"It all seems crazy to me."

"We don't differ about that. Loony came to my mind as the right word. But why not have her in, and ask her to think again?"

"That'll be the best way."

The Superintendent took up the telephone, and a few minutes later Mrs. Nolan was led into the room.

She did not come reluctantly. She looked sullen and short-tempered, but it was the aspect of a woman who had something to say and was in no fear of those to whom she had been given the opportunity of saying it.

She had confessed to a homicide, which, if it did not lead to her own destruction in the more leisurely mode of the law, must be reasonably calculated to lead to imprisonment, probably for a long period. She had foreseen this in a vague way, though, if she had analysed her own anticipations, she had thought rather of giving a momentary cover to Lady Eleanor (surely Mr. Tilson would do *something* to get her out of the danger in which she lay!) rather than of being permanently convicted of the crime to which she had confessed.

Now she came with willing feet, not because she would welcome questions on a statement which she had found difficult to construct, but because she herself had something to say.

"Mrs. Nolan," Superintendent Backhouse began for it had been agreed that the questioning should be left to him—"we want to ask you a few questions upon the statement that you have made. There are one or two things that we think may not have been put down quite accurately."

119

"Before I talk about anything else," she retorted vigorously, "I want to know that I shall be put in a different room."

The two men looked surprised. The accommodation provided at Scotland Yard for such delinquents is of the most modern kind. It may not give more than the minimum of comfort, but it is most careful not to give less.

The Superintendent asked: "Do you know where she's been put?"

"I believe she's in number three."

"Would you say what your grievance is?"

"I'm not going to stand that hole in the door."

Again they looked genuinely surprised. The small grill in the door through which prisoners can be inspected both day and night is so invariable a feature of modern cells that it might be hard to convince a modern warder that prisons existed for thousands of years without that indignity having been invented by some sadistic expert in mental torture. And is it not proverbial wisdom that eels become accustomed to being skinned?

"I'm afraid," he said, "that we can do nothing about that. It is a feature of all the cells. You must try to realise that you haven't come to the Savoy Hotel. What we want to know is how near you were to the table when you struck the blow."

"I've got nothing to say about that."

"But if I were to agree that the grill be covered?"

"Would it stay like that?"

"Yes, as long as you were here."

"Then I'll answer anything that you like to ask. That is, as well as I can."

"Well, I've asked where you were standing."

"I don't remember exactly. I don't think anyone would."

"But you were facing Nolan?"

"Yes, of course."

"And the table was behind you?"

"Yes. Hadn't I just snatched up the knife from it?"

"You know best about that. Anyway, you were facing Nolan, and you had your back to the table?"

"Yes. That was about it."

"Then will you take this ruler and show us just how you dealt the blow?"

She took the ruler in her right hand, and made a vague forward thrust which the two officers regarded in silence.

Superintendent Backhouse asked: "And then Nolan fell over the chair?"

"Yes, of course."

The two men exchanged glances. They both knew that she was lying and Combridge expected his superior officer to put it to her in plain words. But he only said: "I think you've told us all that we need to know," and touched the bell to summon the wardress who would take her back to her cell.

As the door shut, Combridge said: "Well, that's clear enough. But where do we go from here?"

"I don't see that we can do much in view of the bargain that you have made—not for the next few days."

"You think that was a mistake?"

"Not at all. I think it will bring us a confession that will hold together better than the one that we've got now."

"I wonder whether you've got any theory as to what *did* occur?"

"It's something more than theory. I should say there isn't a doubt. Who would go to the top of the table, to take the chair there? Lady Eleanor, of course. How would she stand, when she was pulling the chair a bit sideways to sit down? Facing the table, of course. He must have come up behind her and tried to maul her about in his usual way, and she picked up the knife, and pushed it backwards, at her right side. It went in just as it would if she did that."

"Yes, that sounds reasonable."

"What I'm not sure about is what she really intended to do. You know how soft some parts of the human body are, if you miss the bones. And that knife would go in so easily where it did. It would be like going through butter. But I should say that she reacted too impulsively to have any definite purpose. A good counsel ought to get her off with a year, or even better than that considering what Nolan was, and what he had done to her—and particularly what he had no right to be doing then. But the present question is, what shall we do with his wife, and how what you've said to Tilson will affect his bargain with us?"

"You may be right," the Chief Inspector answered doubtfully. "It sounds like a good guess. But there's something phoney about it all the same. If Lady Eleanor did it, it's no use telling me that she'd marry Tilson without letting him know the truth; and you can't think that he'd marry her, and straightway make a bargain to give her away to us."

"I don't even agree about that. He might think it was now or never, and he'd get the marriage in first, whatever had got to happen afterwards. He's lawyer enough to know that they couldn't keep us waiting for many days more.

121

"He may think also that he'll get her off the more lightly if he's shown his confidence in her by marrying her after she's told him what she did. He meant to have her to himself for a few days, and he's contrived it very cleverly, as a lawyer would."

"The next question's what we're going to do with the one that we've got here."

"Yes, we've either got to go on taking the confession seriously and have her up tomorrow, or prosecute her for making a false statement—public mischief and all that—or—"

"I don't like that public mischief idea. Suppose we were wrong and she had done it, shouldn't we look about the biggest fools that were ever born?

"We prosecute her for saying that she's a murderess, and she defends herself on the ground that she really is, and she's believed, and found not guilty of making a false confession, and then—"

"Yes, I see. You know, Combridge, you've been handling this case excellently, but I think you're losing your nerve, and I'm not sure that you hadn't better leave it to me. The only important question is how what we do may affect your Tilson bargain. We mustn't let that go wrong. And if it goes right, you needn't do much worrying about what will happen to the two who've been trying to hide the truth."

"I'm quite willing to leave it to you."

"Then I say we'd better tell Tilson we're not entirely satisfied with the confession, and we're not keeping her here. That leaves everything as it was, and he'll have no shadow of excuse for not keeping faith with us."

On this decision, he rang up Cole and Tilson, only to learn that Mr. Tilson had gone for the day.

He had no choice but to leave the matter till the next morning and, seeing that, he decided that Lucille might stay where she was in the meantime.

But when morning came he had the satisfaction of hearing Mr. Tilson congratulate him on having made a wise decision, to which he added: "And, by the way, I should be particularly grateful if you'd advise her to give me a call, if possible by midday."

Chastened by her experiment in generous mendacity, Lucille did as she was desired, and when she returned to her employment that afternoon, Charles Tilson had the third signed statement in his safe, which would enable him to fulfil his bargain with Scotland Yard.

CHAPTER XXXIII.

ESCAPE?

CHARLES turned the key in his safe with the satisfaction of knowing that he could keep his contract with the police in a literal way, and that the two who had done so much to protect his wife would be saved from the legal peril they had incurred. That was much. But the central problem remained. Eleanor might be safe for the few days that the bargain covered, but her position would be evil indeed if she were within reach of English laws when her confession was on the file of the C.I.D.

But for good or evil, his plans were made. The apparent levity of the visit to the Adelphi Theatre had been a cloak to a conference with the Truscotts and the enlistment of the assistance of Messrs Fell and Unster, which these plans required; when the four, in almost carefree mood, had had the supper together which often terminates such amusement, they were aware of an agreed conception which, for all its audacity, might end a bad dream in a fairer dawn.

The preliminary difficulty of the flight, as Charles had planned it, was that Eleanor had surrendered her passport, and the promise to return it was unlikely to be honoured now that Mrs. Nolan had been released. But a husband, on his marriage, acquires the right to have his wife entered upon his own, for which an application must now be risked. It was to reduce this hazard that he had arranged that it should be made, not through a travel agency or his own office, but by that of Fell and Unster, a channel through which discovery or interception would be less probable. And this passport, valid and viséd, it would be essential to have.

Discreet enquiries had shown that, though the escape should (and, indeed, must, to have any prospect of success) be made by air, it would be impracticable, even with a privately chartered plane, to make an unbroken journey. The distance was too great for any plane which (with an efficient pilot) could be quietly procured, even apart from the fact that one which could do so great a distance without refuelling could not be landed on a small space. There was hardly a spot in Mabuda which was not broken in surface or densely wooded, and there was the added contingency of landing upon an elephant's back.

For the few days of respite which were theirs, Charles joined his wife in her own home, and it was there that the new passport was delivered by Edith's hands when the hour of decisive action came.

It was on the sixth day by the noon post that Chief Inspector Combridge received an envelope containing the signed statements, and with the name of Charles Tilson as witness on all three.

He glanced over them quickly and saw that all that had been promised had been supplied. He saw also that Superintendent Backhouse had been correct in the guess which he had made, and lost no time in reporting this, with the congratulations which even a Superintendent is pleased to hear.

Superintendent Backhouse was as complimentary in reply. He said: "What is most important is that the course you took has been justified by its results. We know now who committed the crime (not that I think she did anything very bad, but that's strictly between ourselves), and you can get the warrant at once. There's nothing more to be done, the other two being in the clear. But I know you won't lose any time, for you can't expect that Lady Eleanor Tilson is just staying at home, waiting for you to call."

"No, I'm not such a fool as that. Although Tilson may have decided that the game could be played in a worse way. He's got the two others out of the mess they were in—and you'd have said that that would take some doing till he bid in the way he did. He may rely on public sympathy, and—well, you know how much can be said for her, if it be put in the right way."

"That's true enough, but you'll find he'll have thought of something better than that."

"I don't say you're wrong. But he's got to give her up or his own business, if he gets her away now. Of course, as she's a wealthy woman, he might do that, but he wouldn't find it easy, clever though we'll agree that he is. We've got all the airports watched by men who have her photograph, and don't trust to names. They scrutinise everyone going abroad. They've been doing that all the week, though she's never been out of our sight when she's been outside her own door.

"But the fact is they've done nothing so far. They haven't tried to book either by water or air, and it's a bit late to try now."

He spoke confidently, but he was conscious of an opponent he had to respect, and was neither much annoyed nor surprised when he learnt in the next hour that, for the moment at least, Lady Eleanor had evaded those who had been set to watch her, with a deliberation which showed that it must have been part of a detailed plan.

She had left her home at about ten-thirty, using her own car, and had been followed by one containing, besides the driver, three experienced C.I.D. men who were familiar with numerous methods of evasion and adroit to foil them.

She had left her car at the main entrance of an Oxford Street store, from which there were numerous exits; two of the plain-clothes men had got out of a vehicle which remained by her own and followed her closely. Should she leave by another exit, it would be the part of one to continue to keep her under observation, and of the other to hurry back to his companions to report what had occurred.

But what she had done had been to walk out at the back of the premises into a narrow street which had been blocked by numerous delivery vans, go a short distance along it, and get into a car which had evidently been waiting for her, and which moved rapidly away.

It says much for the efficiency, and something for the luck, of her pursuers that they were not shaken off by this method, losing only one man, whom there had been no time to pick up.

But when she entered other similar premises, and they drove rapidly round the building in anticipation of the same procedure, they were defeated by a changed technique, by which she regained the car she had left and disappeared before they could take up the chase. When they found it again, three minutes later, she was no longer within it.

This was telephoned to Scotland Yard with the self-reproaches of men who felt that they were not expected to fail, but found that they were not to blame, for the Chief Inspector knew that, while it is usually possible to keep sight even among crowds of one who does not know that he is followed, it approaches the impossible to do so in a great city, if the quarry be of ordinary intelligence and conscious of the pursuit.

He said: "That can't be helped. But she'll be a clever woman if she can keep it up for forty-eight hours," and then proceeded to throw out the wide net which sets every constable and many newspaper readers upon the chase, to the farthest ends of the land.

After that, he could only wait for news which he did not expect to be long delayed, though the hours must be punctuated by many false reports, probably involving the questioning or detention of innocent individuals who might afterwards be difficult to placate.

125

But it was only mid-afternoon when he had a visitor as unexpected as the news he brought. The telephone rang on his desk, and the voice of Sergeant Hargreaves enquired whether he would see Mr. Victor Bland.

He asked: *"Who?"* and then: "You're not joking, Hargreaves?"

"No, sir. He isn't one you forget."

"Does he say what it's about?"

"It's something to do with the Nolan murder. He won't say more than that. I should bet he's got something to sell."

"Well, send him up."

CHAPTER XXXIV.

THE UNEXPECTED

THE man who entered the Chief Inspector's office was tall, well-dressed, and of a cool assurance sufficient to ignore the fact that when Combridge had seen him last he had been released from a dock which three companions had left by a worse way.

He was still young, and had the air of one who would be equal to holding his own in any company to which he might come, a poised self-assurance that may have been decisive in tilting a doubtful scale when he had been prosecuted for the distribution of forged bank notes, which, he said confidently, he had taken in good faith from men whom he had had no cause to distrust.

A faint doubt in the judge's mind, less of his guilt than of the sufficiency of the legal proof, had become a larger one in the jury-room, and proved sufficient to set him free. But to Combridge he was nothing more or less than a criminal who had defeated the Yard, and for whom they must wait until he came into their hands again. He asked: "You want to see me?" and there was no friendliness in his tone.

"I understand that you are interested in the solution of the Nolan case?"

"So I am. But if you think that there is a mystery that you could help us to solve, I'd better say at once that we've cleared it up."

"Well, if you call a case cleared up before you've made an arrest—"

"It is usual for that to follow without much delay."

Mr. Victor Bland—it was a name which he had given himself, as surely any man should be free to do—rose without showing any sign of annoyance. He said: "I'm not going to offer you anything you don't want."

He was halfway to the door before the Chief Inspector, conscious that he might not be handling the interview in the best way, said with somewhat more courtesy than before: "How can I tell that, while I don't know what your information is?"

He waved his hand to the vacated chair and Mr. Bland occupied it again.

He said: "I'll just ask you one question and if you're not interested we'll let it pass. What would you give for the names on the passports that Mr. and Lady Eleanor Tilson are using now?"

"You mean that they are attempting to get out of the country with forged passports?"

"My question certainly suggested that possibility."

The Chief Inspector answered with careful deliberation: "If you give me the names that are on forged passports by which it will be subsequently shown that they have left or will have attempted to leave this country, we will pay you ten pounds as soon as the fact has been proved."

"Suppose we say fifty?"

"Suppose we say twenty-five."

"I don't haggle. It's fifty or let it go."

"Very well, when we've proved it true."

"You'll put that in writing?"

"You can trust us without that."

"You are not trusting me."

"Perhaps there is a difference."

"And perhaps we differ as to what that difference is."

Mr. Bland still smiled, but he again showed a tendency to rise from his chair, and his opponent, who felt that he was being offered something he must not miss, admitted defeat.

He wrote a short note, at which Mr. Bland gave a quick glance before folding it and putting it into his wallet.

He said: "Mr. Thomas Birchall—you'd better write this down—35 The Crescent, Huddersfield. Viséd for France and Italy. Miss Mary Mitchell, St. Margaret's School, Armley. Same visas."

"Is there a Miss Mitchell?"

"Sure to be. They've been provided by people who know their job. Good quality articles and a good price paid."

"I won't ask you how you came by this information, or who you're giving away, but if it's correct, you can come in a week's time and pick up the cash."

"*Suaviter in modo,*" his visitor said, as he rose for the third time. It was in a mocking tone, but his cheek flushed slightly at an imputation which was in fact quite untrue, but of which he could not logically complain.

"I suppose I've done right," Combridge said dubiously to himself, for he had gone somewhat beyond his personal authority, and he would be awkwardly placed if his action were not approved, though he knew it to be something he had little reason to fear. He thought: "Tilson might get through, if they tried going separately. But she never would. The photos are too good."

He wondered how the solicitor had got into communication with the passport forgers, and then remembered that Cole and Tilson had defended Bland and his less fortunate companions. That was an explanation that went halfway, but left the question of why the solicitor should have been betrayed by the man whom he had defended with such success. Was it possible that the forged documents had been demanded in consideration of what had been done, or of what was known in the solicitor's office, in a way that had been resented, with this result? He knew that the proverb of honour among thieves has little evidence in its support. Anyway, it was a question with which he was not concerned. The reward would not be paid unless the information was true.

He set the telephone to work—several lines at once—to inform those who were watching the airports, railway departure platforms, and ports of embarkation, of the information he had obtained. It brought, almost at once, a report that the passports had been used on one of the smaller airlines, the two passengers having booked separately, but both for Paris. Detective-Sergeant Spencer said that he had not noticed them particularly—why should he have done so?—but he was prepared to swear that no one resembling the photograph he held had boarded a Paris plane. He said that he was confident that he would have seen through any disguise, and he continued this assertion in face of the overwhelming evidence with which he was soon confronted.

CHAPTER XXXV.

ARREST

THE Paris telephone, which became busy for the next hour between the Bureau de Sûreté and Scotland Yard, brought first the expected information that it was too late to detain anyone from a plane which had arrived before the enquiry was made; and then that the two passengers had already left on another one on which they had booked for Khartoum. They had done this openly, as Mr. and Lady Eleanor Tilson, for which a different passport must have been used. Was it a through flight? No, it would call at Rome. There would be time, though not much, to get into communication with the Italian police and have the fugitives taken off there.

It was a matter for quick action, and Combridge, well content with what good luck (if such it were) rather than his own exertions had delivered into his hands, went at once to take counsel and share responsibility with the Superintendent in the next room.

Superintendent Backhouse listened without interruption and then gave his opinion: "It sounds as though you've pulled it off, and what's left is no more than routine, though you've no time to lose.

"I can't see why she's thrown herself into your lap in the way she has. They could have flown a lot further away, in more directions than one. But that's not your worry. I don't see how you can do anything about the forged passports now, as they've stopped using them. They'd take some proving, and they've probably been thrown into the sea on the way to Rome. And it would take time, which you haven't got.

"That lets Tilson out. You can't ask the Italian police to hold him, if his passport's in order. It's not an extraditable offence to take his wife out of the country, even if she is wanted for murder. But I don't suppose he'll go on without her.

"I should guess that they've planned to get off at Rome, and that the booking to Khartoum is a blind. They think they'll keep on changing planes and we shall get left behind. Even a solicitor *might* be as silly as that, especially if he couldn't think of a better way. And, of course, they may have an assortment of passports they haven't used. And why should they go to Khartoum? It's a long way off, without offering any safety to them. Yes, I expect they're reckoning that they'll get off at Rome before you have any idea that they've got away. We mustn't forget that they'll have no idea that Bland's sold them out. They've probably got some hiding hole beyond there. Perhaps a friend's yacht at Naples. Or they might try slipping across the Adriatic. There are some addresses there that might not be quick to open the door when you rang, especially with all the money that Lady Eleanor may have been able to smuggle through.

"But it's no use guessing. The only thing to do is to ask the police there to pick her up, and we'll have any dope they need sent out on the next plane."

"Suppose she doesn't get off? It's a British plane."

"That ought to be a bull point for us. If it were a foreign one, it might raise some awkward questions. But they'll know how to handle that. Toscanini won't let us down. I reckon you've got about a couple of hours, more or less, and if you put a priority call in at once, it should be time enough and to spare."

It was not a matter on which the Chief Inspector was likely to dawdle. In the next hour he talked to the Italian police. He talked to the British Embassy in Rome. He talked to Whitehall. He talked to the British Embassy again, and again to the Italian police.

If it had been by luck that the information had come—and who among us would go far without its assistance?—he would not fail to supply the more positive qualities which deserve success.

And it was soon to appear that the deserved success would not be withheld. When the plane alighted, he heard, the fugitives had made no move to leave it. Actually, they had had little time to attempt it before the police had intruded upon them, and were requiring them to get off, which they very resolutely declined to do.

It appeared that it was a contingency for which Mr. Tilson, though he may not have anticipated it, had not been unprepared. He had the written opinion of an eminent British counsel, with an Italian translation for those whose English might not be equal to its legal phraseology: definitely, they would not move.

But it was made clear to him that nothing would be gained by resistance. The police, polite but emphatic, said that they were prepared to use force if necessary, let international law be what it might. They pointed out that a junior secretary from the British Embassy was present to give sanction for what they did.

Mr. Tilson enquired whether they proposed to use violence against himself—or his wife only? After consultation among themselves, and with the representative of the British Government, they said that it was Lady Eleanor only whom they proposed to arrest. But doubtless Signor Tilson would desire to alight with his wife?

But Signor Tilson replied that he would do nothing—not even that!—to countenance or condone the lawless action which they proposed. What they did should have no remotest shadow of sanction from him.

After that, as the Chief Inspector heard with a grim satisfaction, his wife, with no more than a gesture of force being used, had descended upon Italian soil, while her husband continued his Khartoum flight. What could be the meaning of that? Well, perhaps it had been no more than to emphasise that there had been no yielding by him. He might return on the next day.

After that, it was reported that Lady Eleanor Tilson had said that she had suffered from airsickness so badly that she had been actually pleased to be taken out of the plane. She would not even raise any objection to being sent back to England, providing it were by sea or rail.

It was not a request that could be lightly refused. It involved a slightly slower method of travelling, but what importance could there be in that? And to have refused might have increased sympathy for one who already had more than could be officially approved.

The reply was that an officer would be flown out at once, who would bring her back by rail.

But Combridge was still warily alert for a hidden trap. He enquired: had she made any attempt to get any legal aid? Was there any indication that the short delay would be used to set any legal procedure in motion such as might obstruct her return? Being assured that she had done nothing in that direction, he became easier in mind.

With a sense of poetic justice, he selected Sergeant Spencer, who was no longer required to watch airplane departures, for the duty of bringing her back. He would be able to see for himself the lady who had escaped his vigilance, and put a black mark against his record which it would not be easy to wipe away. He was to be accompanied by a Sergeant Willows, a female member of the C.I.D., so that the proprieties might be observed. They were to leave for Rome in two hours.

The Chief Inspector was to be glad afterwards that he had done nothing to sanction any needless delay, apart from the main concession, for which he could not reasonably be blamed.

Having completed these arrangements, he had some justification for feeling that the case was taking a satisfactory course, and that for the moment there was nothing more to be done.

The prisoner would soon be on the way home. The three statements—including her own—which would so clearly convict her were in the safe. He had a right to feel tired, and that he had done enough for the day.

He was delayed, as he was on the point of leaving, by the appearance of Mr. Bland, who wished to know whether the seven days were to be literally observed to the last hour, or was he satisfied that the fifty pounds had been fairly earned? It was a question to which he felt there could be only one reply. He authorised the payment and went home to bed.

He would have been greatly puzzled, and less content, had he known that Victor Bland had received the same amount from Mr. Cole a few hours before.

CHAPTER XXXVI.

SERGEANT SPENCER THINKS
THERE IS SOMETHING WRONG

CHIEF INSPECTOR COMBRIDGE was still asleep (it being Sunday morning) when his telephone rang. Scotland Yard was on the phone to Rome, and the call was being transferred to him. The next moment he heard Spencer's voice: "Well, sir, she's here safe enough, and the johnnies here say that they've got instructions to waive extradition proceedings, and I can bring her back as soon as I like. But there's something phoney about it that I thought you ought to know."

"I don't see how there can be. We can't ask more than—"

"It isn't that, sir. It's the girl herself. She's as much like her photo as a cat's like a mutton chop."

"Well, you know what photos are. But I thought that one was rather good. If you're trying to excuse yourself for letting her get away, you might have left it till you got back."

"It isn't only the photo, sir. It's the description you circulated. Is she a brunette or a blonde?"

"She was a brunette when I saw her last."

"Well, she isn't now. And what about height?"

"She's about five feet three."

"Then she's lost three inches."

"You're not telling me they've taken off the wrong woman?"

"No. I don't see how they could. They say she was seated with Mr. Tilson. And, of course, he was asked to produce his passport, and they checked on the photo there. I think the mistake must have been in the one that was issued to me."

"Well, I don't. Does she admit that she's Lady Eleanor Tilson?"

"She doesn't deny it. She just won't talk. But there's something wrong somewhere."

134

"Well, you must bring her back by the next train, and we'll see what we've got when she gets here. I suppose she's wearing a wedding ring?"

"Yes."

"Well, that's something. It shows she's somebody's wife, and she's most likely to be married to the man she was with."

Giving himself this rather meagre encouragement, the Chief Inspector hung up and faced the problem which the conversation had raised. Was it possible that the solicitor, after marrying Lady Eleanor, had bolted with another woman within a week? Improbability approached the absurd. And yet something was wrong. He supposed that Lady Eleanor must have dyed her hair, which would not be very surprising, in view of the position in which she stood. It was natural that she should attempt disguise, and he might have been told no more than that it had been successfully done. But as to height? Well, no one should be exact about that, with only memory for a guide. Probably the whole explanation was that Spencer was making the best defence he could for having been fooled by a bottle of dye, or perhaps a wig?

He went to sleep again, with this comforting theory uppermost in his mind, but he woke to the consciousness that he was a puzzled and worried man.

CHAPTER XXXVII.

A SURPRISE FOR THE CHIEF INSPECTOR

IT HAS been allowed that the Chief Inspector was not always quick-witted, but, as Mr. Jellipot had observed more than once, he was very far from being a fool.

Now he had a sound conviction that something was wrong, though he could not guess what.

That the Tilsons should have avoided observation by leaving separately, and with forged passports, was natural enough; and that Lady Eleanor should have disguised herself appeared likely also—a precaution which her husband might have felt that he had less reason to take, in view of that separation, and the fact that there was no ground on which he could have been legally detained.

And the fact that they had preferred to continue the journey from Paris together in their own names, and with an authentic passport, might also be considered explicable, as he certainly would not have been able to act in time to intercept them, had they not been betrayed by Bland.

Then what was causing the disquiet which he now felt? If Lady Eleanor had disguised herself well enough to pass Sergeant Spencer's experienced eyes at the airport, might she not have repeated that success now? Well, it was possible. But no one who knew Spencer would put it higher than that.

Was it natural that the solicitor should continue his journey when the police had removed his wife? Well, that was possible also. They might have quarrelled half an hour earlier! But possible was the most that could be conceded. Beyond any certain knowledge, his experienced instinct told him that it had all been too easy—and too queer.

The day being Sunday, there was no opportunity for further action but much for thought, and it is a tribute to the thoroughness of his methods that he resolved to telephone the Passport Office next morning, and ask to inspect their file relating to the passport which Mr. Tilson must have procured during the short time following his marriage, with the photographs which it would contain. He calculated that Sergeant Spencer and his prisoner would arrive shortly after noon, and he wished to be as fully informed as possible beforehand.

He reached Scotland Yard on Monday rather earlier than his usual hour, feeling that it was a fifty-fifty chance that he would be receiving the commendations of his superiors before the day closed, or be exposed to them as a complete fool. Even without knowledge of Mr. Bland's complicated activities, he had become sensitive to the methods which were being employed against him.

It was eleven-forty-five when the passport papers and photographs were laid on his desk, and one glance at these was sufficient to tell him that his worst fear lagged behind the fact, and that he knew exactly what to expect when Sergeant Spencer arrived.

He picked them up and went into Superintendent Backhouse's office.

"Look at these," he said bitterly, as he laid them down. "That tricky lawyer's made monkeys of us, and for all we know, Lady Eleanor may be in Greenland by now."

But the Superintendent declined to rise to his temperature. He looked at the photographs with interest. "Not a bad-looking girl," he said. "Do you happen to know who she is?"

"Know? I should think I do. She's Miss Westerham—Mrs. Truscott—of course."

"Yes, I suppose I should have guessed that. And, of course, you took the watch off the airports and other exits when you thought that Lady Eleanor had got through?"

"Yes, you needn't rub it in. I know what a fool I've been."

"I wouldn't put it that high. But you can't call them a dull lot. And Tilson has played very fairly with us. Have you thought that you know now who the murderess is, and we've got evidence enough to convict in our own hands? It's become only a matter of catching her, and we mayn't be too slow for that."

The words were hardly spoken when Sergeant Spencer and his prisoner entered the room.

Edith, with Spencer on one side of her, and a policewoman on the other, had the confident smile of one who anticipates giving her opponents a most unwelcome surprise, which she had wit enough to perceive that she did not do.

"Will you tell us, Mrs. Truscott," Superintendent Backhouse asked, "why you have done this?"

She showed courage and resource in the quickness with which she adjusted her mind to what she had to meet, and was adroit to avoid the trap.

"Don't you think that's a rather cool question," she retorted, "when I've been brought here practically by force? It seems to me I haven't done anything. I've been done to."

"You know perfectly well what I mean. You're only here because you masqueraded as Lady Eleanor Tilson; and if you did that to defeat the ends of justice—which is the only reasonable explanation—you may find yourself in a very serious position."

"But I haven't masqueraded at all. And if anyone had asked who I was before fetching me off the plane, how do you know that I shouldn't have said at once? Though I don't think I should have been believed if I had."

"You won't deny that you travelled with a false passport?"

"Of course I do. I wasn't asked to show a passport at all, and if I had been, I shouldn't have done it. You know perfectly well that you've got mine yourselves—and then you complain that it wasn't in my own bag."

"Will you try to realise that this is a serious matter and that verbal quibbling won't get you anywhere? We have your signed statement that you know that Lady Eleanor Tilson killed Nolan. Will you tell us in a straightforward way where you think she is now?"

"You mean you don't know?" she retorted, with as much of incredulous mockery in her voice as she could contrive. "Then it's not likely I do. I couldn't do more than a poor guess, and you might do better. But I'm not going to be turned off like that. What I want is to have my solicitor here. You can't say that that's more than I've a right to ask. And then I'll answer anything that he says I may."

Since the appearance of the police on the Italian airport had shown her that Victor Bland had done his part successfully, she had reckoned that every moment's delay that she could contrive might be vital in its result. She had won, she supposed, much time when she had pleaded imaginary airsickness to avoid the speedier method of return, and she spoke now with the same aim.

But the Superintendent saw the position in exactly the same light. He said: "There's no need for you to have your solicitor here, because you can go to him. We're not going to keep you here. But you've asked for any trouble you've had, and if you hear no more of it, you'll be about the luckiest young woman who's ever put her tongue out at the law. But I'm not promising that. We'll see how things go from now."

He picked up a telephone, and gave a brief order that Mrs. Truscott's passport ("name's Westerham, of course, on that") should be returned to her, and told Sergeant Spencer to show her the door.

As she left, with the feeling that she had encountered an unwelcome efficiency and a doubt (which went beyond the fact) of how long they had known her identity, and how much delay her tactics had really caused, Superintendent Backhouse said: "It was no use wasting time with her. If she'd told us anything, it would only have been to make fools of us again. But Truscott may have sense enough to warn her not to make any more trouble. I shouldn't wonder if he's more concerned as to how far his own firm has gone off the rails already. We've let the woman slip through our fingers, no doubt with another of Bland's extra specials to show, and now Khartoum is the only clue."

"I don't see much in that. He'll have had lots of time to get out of there. He may be in Cape Town now or Ceylon."

"So he may. But isn't it more likely that he has waited there for her to join him?"

"No, I think they'd be more likely to arrange a meeting elsewhere. They're too wily to make it as simple as that."

"Perhaps so. But we've got to think it out on their lines. They've got to try to end up where extradition treaties don't apply, and the question is where it is most likely to be, with Khartoum as the first step. They'll want to go quickly to earth. I should say there'll still be a good chance, if we lose no time. You'd better get through to the F.O., and ask what they'd advise anyone to do, if they wanted to show them a way out."

It was done at once, and in half an hour they had been told much more than they had expected to hear. For they had learnt not only that Mabudaland was the nearest possible refuge (of which the world held very few), but that information had just been received that Mr. Charles Tilson was taking up an appointment there. The Chief Inspector felt that Fortune was at last giving her favours to him, as she often would when the last hand came to be played.

CHAPTER XXXVIII.

THE PRINCIPLE OF RECIPROCITY

"IT'S JUST possible," the Chief Inspector said with obvious truth, "that she isn't going to join him before he gets to Mabudaland. She may be making her own way separately there, or they may have planned for her to lie up somewhere else, and all this humbug has been intended to give her time to go somewhere to ground."

"Yes, or pigs might fly; but it isn't a possibility about which a butcher worries his mind. We've got to bank on Tilson and begin at Khartoum, while that cheeky hussy goes to her lawyer husband and they both laugh at the mugs we've been. Well, there's a proverb about who laughs last, and it applies to us more often than not. We must see what we can do now."

But Mrs. Truscott was not on the way to her lawyer husband, for, after a short telephone conversation with him at the booth which is less than a hundred yards from the headquarters of the C.I.D., she had taken a taxi to the offices of Messrs Cole and Tilson, where she had been told that the senior partner was anxious to see her.

"I suppose Eleanor will be all right by now?" she enquired, as Mr. Cole greeted her cordially and she sat down at the side of his desk.

"So we may hope, or at least that she's well on the right way; though it's always a mistake to halloo before you're out of the wood. But if she is, it's thanks to Mrs. Nolan and you, and she wants me to make it clear that she isn't ungrateful for what you've done."

"I don't want anything from her, if you mean that. I think it's been rather fun."

"It is a very sensible way in which to regard it. But in fact what has been proposed will be further favours to her, though there may be advantages on both sides.

"In the case of Mrs. Nolan, I have already fixed up that her firm will control the exporting of machinery and other merchandise to

Lady Eleanor's new home, which they will be very much more competent to do than either of our two black friends at the Mabudaland Embassy. It will mean very substantial business for them. And you may be interested to hear that Mrs. Nolan's stake in the firm will be solidified by the fact that she is marrying its managing director almost at once. She was fair enough to observe that Lady Eleanor's energetic use of the carving knife had been very beneficial to her in that direction, as, though she might have taken divorce proceedings (about which she had made a difficulty for herself of which we both know), and had considered the possibility of taking the risk of such action, she might have gained little advantage from her legal freedom, as the gentleman she is intending to marry belongs to a Church which does not approve of divorce."

"Well it only shows what a lot of good might be done if the law were not always so officious to interfere. There ought to be some way of avoiding the sort of mess that we've had to find a way through. Why shouldn't there be a law that if anyone should kill anyone else he could get acquitted by putting in twelve affidavits that it was a good thing rather than not?"

"It is an idea which certainly has the quality of originality. Why not put it to Mr. Jellipot, and see what can be done?"

"Well, I might do worse. He wouldn't be one to turn it down just because of its being new. But I expect he'd want too many qualifications to make it work. Anyway, I don't suppose I shall go back there. I shall have to think about getting a home."

"I was coming to that. Lady Eleanor left her residence in Belfield Gardens rather abruptly, and she is anxious that her effects should be in friendly hands, and that her home should not be broken up. She contemplates (if she should be successful in getting away) that a time may come when she will be able to return, and she would like in that event to feel that she could come back to her own home.

"She has given me a general power of attorney to act on her behalf, and she has authorised me to make this offer—or rather request—to you.

"I will convey her residence and its contents absolutely to you, free of charge, on the sole condition that, should she return to England at any time and wish to resume possession, you will return them to her in the same condition—within reasonable bounds—as you will have received them from her, for which she will then make you a payment of £7,000."

"It is an absurdly generous offer. She would be paying me for her own property."

"That is one point of view. But you will see that, both in what has been done for Mrs. Nolan and is being offered to you, a principle of reciprocity has been observed, so that you need have no hesitation whatever in accepting; and in any case she has been and must remain under a great obligation to you."

"Oh, I don't mind accepting! And it's a lovely home to have. Of course, if Edward agrees."

"I have already put the matter to Mr. Truscott, who hoped that you might be pleased to accept."

"Then that's settled. You don't think that I've got anything more to fear from the police?"

"I should think it extremely unlikely. The way in which they were hoaxed is not a matter which they will be anxious to expose to public derision. The—inaccurate—passport was issued to Mr. Tilson, not to yourself. There are other legal complexities which we need not discuss in detail, but you may like to know that I have exchanged views with Mr. Jellipot upon the whole situation, and in the improbable—he has called it the extremely improbable—event of the police taking any further action against you, he will undertake your defence."

"Then I shall be silly to give it another thought. But I shall have to go now, for I arranged to meet Edward for a late lunch after coming here, and he must have been waiting about an hour."

"You mean you haven't had lunch yet? Then you must indeed forgive me for the intrusion of less urgent matters."

CHAPTER XXXIX.

A POLICY OF SUSPENSE

THE C.I.D. is not easily foiled. Charles Tilson had recognised this from the first, but the knowledge could do no more than to make him wary of perils he could not shun.

He knew that the fugitive murderer usually makes his capture certain by attempting to leave the country through channels which it is simple to watch, and that there is little more to be done than to pick him out of the trap into which he will surely walk. He would be less easy to capture if he did no more than change his lodgings by the distance of half a mile.

By the elaborate device of the faked exit, and by use of the criminal client his firm had defended successfully, both to provide the bogus passports required and to mislead the police by an apparent betrayal of Charles himself, he had won a trick, but he knew that it was no more than that. He had won a battle, not a campaign, and the harder fight was before him now.

He had so contrived that there had been a period, however short, during which the watch had been relaxed sufficiently for Eleanor to leave the country under conditions which had become merely hazardous, rather than suicidal.

He knew that the police would have become aware of this as soon as they saw the way in which their vigilance had been duped They would guess that the interval had been used, almost certainly with another passport from the Bland factory, and that Lady Eleanor Tilson would be abroad. But where?

So Combridge asked himself, as he arranged that the solicitor, still at Khartoum, should be watched every instant that he was outside his room. He spoke to no one without being observed. The few letters he wrote, including one to Mrs. Truscott, were intercepted and read. But no evidence was found that he was in communication with Eleanor, or she with him. In his letter to Edith, there was no allusion to her. There was only regret that Edith should have left the plane when she did, and a suggestion of what good times might otherwise have been theirs together. "Probably meant for us to read," Chief Inspector Combridge commented sourly, when the copy was on his desk.

Khartoum was searched in vain. No woman entered it, by whatever method or route, without such scrutiny as established definitely that she was not the one who was sought.

So the weeks passed, until the news came that Charles had flown to Latuki, making it probable that he would reach Mabudaland at his next hop, though it could not be done by air. But would he do it alone? Was it possible that his wife was already there?

Those who watched the difficult and limited routes by which its remoteness might be reached were confident that she was not. But no diligence of police, no enquiries of worldwide range, had found the one place where she must certainly be.

Yet what she had done had been simple in its conception, and (for one to whom lack of money was no obstacle) very simple to do.

When she had left her car and become lost in a London crowd, she had taken a 73 bus and gone to an address in Tottenham Court Road, where a young impersonator named (or perhaps we should say, who called herself) Myrtle Starleigh had received her with such hospitality as her resources, aided by a very liberal cheque, had enabled her to provide.

Eleanor had stayed here for two days and had heard the voice of experienced wisdom affirm that, for purposes of disguise, "a man changes his face, but a woman changes her clothes," and had found that (with the aid of cosmetics skilfully used, and different dressing of hair) it was surprisingly true.

By their means (to which the assistance of some padding must be acknowledged), an Englishwoman, the wife of a Rotterdam lawyer, left the house with the Dutch passport which her marriage required her to use, but found no occasion to show it while she travelled on a night coach to Glasgow, and then to Belfast by sea.

As she went on board a boat there which was setting out for a pleasure cruise in Scandinavian waters, it received its first indifferent inspection from busy officials whose minds were on an absconding banker of Austrian origin, which she obviously could not be.

If she were so entranced with Norwegian scenery that she must have her baggage taken ashore, having decided to sacrifice her ticket for a closer acquaintance with its attractions, was there any cause for surprise in that?

Or would it excite remark that she should travel from there to Holland, in view of her husband's name, and the address which her passport bore?

And after that, might not the wife of a Rotterdam lawyer, staying at an Amsterdam hotel, book passage on a liner sailing to the Dutch East Indies without enquiry as to why she should be travelling in that direction?

So the weeks passed, and when the travel-fond Dutchwoman, now accompanied by a Sumatran maid who did not doubt her identity (though she had observed rather more of the makeup that the character required than she had been intended to see), booked a passage to East Africa, her passport, with its multiple authentic stamps and visas, was itself almost conclusive evidence that it would be absurdity to suggest that she and Lady Eleanor Tilson were one.

Very, very nearly, when she arrived at Latuki, she had come to a simple absolute triumph, such as would have completed the mockery of the C.I.D. which they had already found so difficult to digest; but it was by the malice of circumstance that Sergeant Spencer had been flown out, with a plain hint that quick promotion would follow his arrest of the fugitive, and had put up at the modest hotel at which she booked a room she did not intend to use for the night. For, though he had been acquitted of having overlooked her before, the accusation still rankled in his efficient mind, and if a female Eskimo had entered the town, he would not have passed her at the first glance as being other than whom he sought.

CHAPTER XL.

THE CHASE

ELEANOR studied the telephone directory. She wrote down the name of the Clydesdale Travel Agency, and dialled one which was similar, but not quite the same. She said: "Is that the Clydesdale Agency? Wrong number? Oh, so sorry. It must be the heat."

She rang off, dialled the correct number, and asked them to send a prospectus of local tours.

Charles, to whom she had first spoken, knew that the time for action had come. He had recognised her voice, but, more certain than that, she had spoken the code words agreed between them: "It must be the heat."

Sergeant Spencer had been in the billiard room when the Dutch lady and her maid had booked in. Even detective officers must relax at times. Consequently, he did not see her arrive. But he inspected the register half an hour later. When he read the entry, he did not think that he was on the right track, but he left nothing to chance.

The lady kept to her room (where she had lunch served) for the next two hours, but the maid came to the dining room, and sat down modestly at a small vacant table near to the door from which meals were served. It was laid for two, and Spencer joined her a few minutes later, as one who takes his own seat. It was not until the soup plates had been removed that he even gave her a glance.

She was petite, well and quietly dressed, not a usual type of Asiatic, but faintly olive-skinned. Clearly not a European, in a country where racial distinctions had an importance that an Englishman might be slow to understand.

It was different from anything she had experienced in her native land, and something of which she was already acutely and uncomfortably aware. Had she been alone, she would probably have been told at the reception counter that the hotel was full.

It did not surprise her that the strange white man showed no consciousness of her existence at first. Indeed, an abrupt advance would have been almost certainly misunderstood. But when he made an excuse to speak to her later in a casual way and gave her a friendly smile, conversation was only limited by her restricted knowledge of the one language that he could use.

He learned that her mistress was English, which roused him to greater alertness than might have been the case had he first seen her in her well-established disguise. He learnt that she had won the maid's affection and that she was a wealthy woman, with features suggestive of the identity of the girl he sought. He got a vague impression of one who was younger than she would have appeared, of a reticence of conduct, of something held back. He got no further—the language barrier, and the fact that he could not disclose the purpose of his questions, thwarting curiosity—but he had learnt enough to become acutely alert, and when he saw the lady appear in the lounge, dressed for the street, its effect was a sharp disappointment that she was so much less like Lady Eleanor Tilson than he had hoped she would be.

The hotel register lay open on the counter. The hotel was run by a very limited staff in its higher grades. The clerk was not in his place. The detective strolled over and read the number of Mrs. Van de Graaf's room. Boldly, as though it were his own, he mounted to it. Entering, he looked round at cases half unpacked, at a silk dressing gown on the bed. He concluded that, if the lady were going out, she would certainly return. He could not be expected to guess that that was precisely what he was intended to think, that he looked on that which was being thrown away in the cause of successful flight, and to supply the means for returning the maid to her own land, if she should wish to go. It was through the same thought that a wallet of notes lay on the table, from which her wages could be disbursed.

Charles Tilson's elaborate and costly planning did not prevent, but somewhat prolonged, the chase; for the detective, descending again unobserved, after a brief and futile search of the room, and learning from her maid that she had gone to shop in the town, but was returning for dinner, did not doubt the accuracy of the forecast, and was at first disposed to leave further investigation until the evening. But in the next half hour it occurred to him that if she should prove to be the woman he sought, and discovery made by others before he had suggested the possibility, he would be discredited in consequence; on which he called up a colleague who was watching the solicitor's movements. He said: "There's a young woman here, with a Dutch name, Van de Graaf, who's gone out till evening. I've talked to her maid, and I think you ought to be on the alert to see whether she makes any attempt to talk to Tilson, or he with her. I'll check on her thoroughly when she gets back."

Inspector Rawlings said "O.K., Spencer. Thanks for the hint. He's gone to lunch now as usual, but I'll just give him a look-see."

Charles had gone to lunch in his car. He went daily to a place about a quarter of a mile from his hotel. He was usually away for less than an hour. Inspector Rawlings had ceased to follow him out and in. There was nothing singular in his having a car, or using it for so short a distance. Cars in Latuki were considered as necessary as shoes in London. He had bought a small, shabby saloon car with a good engine, that being the only feature about which he had cared, though he had talked about other points.

While he lunched, he parked it at the rear of the snack bar where he took a modest meal. It was out of sight of the road, but in a position he could overlook.

He saw Eleanor pass behind it, and she did not appear on the further side. He knew she had got in, and rose at once. He stuffed his pockets with such food as he could reach, for which he laid down a note in excessive payment. He had feared to pack anything into the car, lest it should be observed. He was taking little away beyond such things as his pockets held, and Eleanor's position must be alike. But the time for concealment had gone. They could rely only on speed.

The Mabudaland boundary was about two hundred miles away. There were four hours of daylight left. The road would be rough from the first, and would get worse.

He saw that Eleanor was in the back seat, and gave her a quick glad word of greeting, but his hand was for the steering wheel, his eyes for the road. Rapidly, though not smoothly, their flight began.

CHAPTER XLI.

WITH NIGHT AHEAD

THE CAR bumped on with no sign of pursuit behind. They saw a farmstead with enclosed land in a wire fence, and a village of native huts, among which women moved or sat and children ran. They came to a filling station and pulled up for the precaution of extra petrol.

A short, brown-bearded man served them genially. He was disposed to talk. Mabudaland?—about a hundred and eighty miles ahead. They had thought less than that. They thought they had done at least thirty miles already. No, they had done twenty-two. What did they intend to do during the night? Go on? It could not be done. They would soon find that there would be no sufficient track to be seen in the dark. Had they thought of the cold? He sold them an old rug. And were they armed? They must not be surprised should they be investigated by an inquisitive lion. He offered to sell them an old shotgun. Charles said he was not an expert shot. He was told that that did not matter at all. The local lions understood firearms. The noise would be enough. But he should avoid hitting the lion. A wounded lion may lose his temper and become dangerous.

He was so friendly that Eleanor ventured to tell him that they feared pursuit. Could he misdirect those who might follow? No, he said: not that he was unwilling, but there was only one road.

"Still," he said, with a grin, "you never know." He threw some broken glass onto the track. It made no difference, but it showed the right feeling, and the interlude had been pleasant, though hurried.

They came to another filling station before dark. They were now in untamed, thinly populated country, but the station, otherwise primitive, had a telephone wire. They asked for enquiry to be made of their brown-bearded friend. Were they being pursued? Yes, they certainly were: police car, with four men armed, making good speed. It must be close behind them by now.

They went on faster, and taking more bumps, than before. They were glad when the darkness came.

They spent the night a mile away from the track, warmly enough under the rug, being together on the back seat. It was a moonless night, but brilliant with stars. The lions left them alone.

CHAPTER XLII.

So Near, and Yet—

IT WAS undulating, park-like country, very thinly wooded, which, to myopic eyes, such as would not observe distinction of boscage, nor a fleeing herd of high-leaping antelopes on the horizon, might have been accepted as English scenery. It was not mountainous, but mile by mile, it rose steadily.

The sky was cloudless, the sun powerful, but the heat was not intense.

The four men in the car had no thought for scenery or temperature. They were conscious only of bumps and jerks as they made the utmost speed they could, which was not much, on a road which was now no more than a narrow foot track, easy to see, but often no more than two feet wide between hillock or hollow, with which their vehicle was not designed to contend.

The driver's eyes had to be on the road, but the three others looked ahead. They watched for a saloon car which they expected every moment to see. Their orders were to bring back the Tilsons, dead or alive. They were to pursue them to the Mabudaland border, but not beyond. How they were to know when they reached it, they had not been told, because it would not have been easy to say. But they had made a rough calculation that it could not now be more than twenty-five miles ahead. They saw the car, which stood motionless, leaning over on its near side.

They discovered on reaching it that a front wheel had sunk into a rocky crevice and become wedged. It was obvious that it could not go forward. An attempt to back up it might have been the explanation of a torn and deflated tyre.

They felt an engine which was still warm. They looked round and saw little cover. It might be possible to hide, but would be very difficult to move unobserved.

151

They decided that the flight must have been continued on foot, and could not have covered much ground. Certainly it should be possible to overtake their quarry before they could reach the sanctuary which they sought. There might have been unspoken thoughts that an invisible boundary might (for a few miles at least) be excusably overlooked. But was it likely that there would be occasion for that? Anticipating success, they continued pursuit, which surely could not be long.

Half an hour later, they came upon those they sought. They sat on a large stone, eating sandwiches. But between them and a halted car there were two great boulders on either side of the way, on which the words had been roughly but plainly painted: "MABUDA BOUNDRY."

"We would offer you some," Charles said, "but we've only got two more, and we don't know how far we shall have to walk."

Captain Dickson hesitated and shrugged his shoulders. He would have taken a risk, but beyond a boundary so clearly marked he had no licence to go. And he had no animus towards those he pursued. Every man prefers success to failure, but it was not a matter on which any blame could be his. Observing a very black and unclad woman who watched them from a distance of about thirty yards, his decision was made that there was nothing more he could be expected to do. He was magnanimous enough to donate a bottle of mineral water to those who must complete their journey on foot, however far it might be. "But I don't suppose," he said, with his eyes on the watching woman, "that your friends will take much finding."

They said they hoped he was right, as they heard him give orders to turn the car, which it was not easy to do. But there was little hope in their hearts, for they supposed the boundary of the land they sought to be still twenty miles ahead.

As the car disappeared in the distance, Eleanor said: "It was lucky they didn't feel the paint, or see the dirt on our hands." (For they had had to roll one of the boulders into the required position.)

Charles answered: "Oh, it soon dries in this sun. But it was your idea of spelling boundary in a new way that made sure we should win the trick. Who would think that that could have been done by us?"

ABOUT THE AUTHOR

SYDNEY FOWLER WRIGHT (1874-1965) penned over seventy volumes of science fiction, fantasy, classic mysteries, historical novels, poetry, and non-fiction, many of them being published by the Borgo Press Imprint of Wildside Press.